CAPTAIN SWING

CAPTAIN SWING

larry duplechan

ALYSON PUBLICATIONS
LOS ANGELES

Typeset and printed in the United States of America.

Published by Alyson Publications Inc.,
P.O. Box 4371, Los Angeles, California 90078.

This book is printed on acid-free paper.

First edition: October 1993
First Alyson paperback edition: April 1996

5 4 3 2 1

ISBN 1-55583-361-6

Library of Congress Cataloging-in-Publication Data

Duplechan, Larry
    Captain Swing: a novel/ Larry Duplechan — 1st ed.
        p.   cm.
    ISBN 1-55583-234-2 (cloth): $15.95
    ISBN 1-55583-361-6 (pbk.): $9.95
    1. Gay men—United States—Fiction   I. Title.
 PS3554.U55C37 1993
813'.54—dc20

ACKNOWLEDGMENTS

The author would like to thank the following for their advice and assistance: Greg Harvey, Michael Denneny, Keith Kahla, Lloyd Duplechan, Wendy G. Glenn, Alan U. Schwartz, Phil Loebach, and Ken Slater.

*To the memory of Alan Cumbey,
Ken Dawson, Wef Fleischman, Don Fusco,
John Medlin, David Sebulski, Gary Steele,
Steve Witner, and Mark Yetter.*

And to Vernita Magee ... because I said I would.

1.

There I go there I go there I go There, I go.
The voice of Eddie Jefferson — a well-worn
whisky baritone, a cello played with an
emery file — poured out of the Walkman headset into
my ears like cocoa into a mug, filling my head with
warm, bittersweet jazz. I sucked in a long, deep yoga
breath, attempting to take "Moody's Mood for Love" into
my body along with the lungfuls of air-conditioned
Prana (life force to a Hindu, just plain air to the average
Joe); then slowly exhaled carbon dioxide, a brief six-
teenth-note sax run, and less than one-zillionth of the
nervous tension that had knotted my shoulders up
around my ears and rendered the palms of both my
hands moist and cold against the leatherette armrests
of my narrow economy-class seat. The window seat to
my right was vacant; still, I kept the center armrest
down — I needed something to clutch.

I slowly shrugged my stiffened shoulders upward,
then pushed them down; opened my eyes, leaned over
and peered out the little porthole of a window. I thought
of that scene from *The Rose*: Bette Midler as the
drugged-out rock 'n' roll diva stares out the window of
her private jet and says, "Where am I? I don't even know

where the fuck I am. All these fuckin' clouds look just alike." I think of that scene at least once every time I find it necessary to strap myself into an airplane.

I hate to fly. Always have. I experience a constant, relentless case of stomach-tightening nerves for the duration of any flight, every flight, takeoff to landing. Lighted signs notwithstanding, I remove my seat belt only to go to the rest room. The rational knowledge that more people die in automobile accidents, from gunshot wounds, and probably from slipping on the soap in the bathtub than in plane crashes does not help. I never claimed it was a rational fear.

I stared out at the thick, foamy carpet of clouds, God's shaving cream suspended across the sky. And I thought, Ice cream castles my ass — all those clouds *do* look just alike. And I hadn't the first idea where I was. Except somewhere high above some spot between Los Angeles and Louisiana. It was a trip I'd made many times before. But not in years, and never in a plane.

Sometimes we drove. In the big, black '60 Chevy, its rear end nearly scraping the pavement from the combined weight of my family's collective rear ends and the luggage in the trunk. And later in the Chevy Caprice — the Blue Bomb, blue as the sky through which the 707 now traveled so precariously, a midsixties Detroit dreammobile with matching blue fabric tuck-and-roll upholstery and the precious air-conditioning that made the drive through interminable hell-hot stretches of Arizona, New Mexico, and Texas almost bearable. We'd leave "before day in the morning" (as Clara said), Lance at the wheel, Clara riding shotgun, two ashy-legged, nappy-headed, rusty-butt boys — my brother David and me — nodding and dozing in the backseat.

Come midday, we munched cold fried chicken and slices of Wonder Bread, Clara feeding Lance with her fingers as he drove. David and I peed in a plastic-lidded coffee can when Nature called where no rest stops or service stations loomed. After some fourteen or fifteen hours on the road, we had generally made San Antonio, where we'd stay the night in some tiny Texas motel, often after one or two false stops at places where "Vacancy" signs proved misleading once a black family stepped toward the check-in desk.

Some twenty-five years after the event, I still carry with me (along with my other many and varied pieces of emotional baggage) the vivid memory of the way one particular desk clerk — a middle-aged woman with turkey wattles beneath her chin and a wiglet of curls that didn't quite match her own hair color — looked down her angular nose and over her half-circle eyeglasses at my father, as if he were a life-size sculpture made of horse manure, and said, "I'm sorry, we have no rooms for you." "The sign out front said 'Vacancy,'" Lance had said. "I'm sorry," the clerk repeated, "we have no rooms here for you." Her meaning was clear even to a boy not yet ten years old.

Sometimes, at least half the time, we'd make the trip by train, eating flat-tasting dinners in the dining car and sleeping Dramamine-heavy sleep in our semi-reclining seats, David and I enduring Lance's rough washcloth baths as we stood in the chrome-and-mirrored men's rest room. Every year, at Christmastime or in the summer, sometimes both, my family would pack up and go to Louisiana to visit the folks they'd left behind. "Loowayzeeana," David pronounced it until he was seven or eight years old. "Home," Clara called it.

"Naw, honey," she'd say to someone on the phone. "We won't be around come Christmas. We're goin' Home." She always seemed to say it with a capital *H*.

Even as a child, I never quite understood how a grown woman with a husband, two sons, and a two-bedroom house of her own could refer to a place halfway across the country as "Home." For me, once I'd left Clara and Lance for college, home was wherever I happened to be living — any one of a succession of largely interchangeable dorm rooms and increasingly comfortable apartments, and finally a two-bedroom house of my own. For Clara, home was obviously where her mother lived; and, to my disadvantage, she expected her children to feel the same way.

Well into my twenties, Clara would call every week or so and say, "When you comin' home?" Finally, she caught me in one of my all-too-frequent sarcastic bitch moods — and I answered her, in what Clara sometimes referred to as my uppity college-boy tone of voice, "Mother, I am home. I'll come see you at your home as soon as I can." By that time, my home was wherever Keith was.

A memory weaved its way in through the music coming from my headset, and washed over me like a warm wave, like sliding into a bath:

Keith lifting me up in his big, bodybuilder arms and carrying me, kicking and giggling like a teenage girl, over the threshold of our empty, just-bought house. The warmth of his body. The solid male muscle of him. The delicious sweat-and-Aramis-cologne smell of him.

The fleeting thought of Keith had barely dissipated before the too-familiar steel claw that had encircled my heart for a solid year squeezed, just enough to remind me it was still there. I shut my eyes tight, bit my lip, and waited out the pain. A long moment passed before I opened them. I turned to the window again — bad idea — and watched the plane's wing flex and sway in the breeze like a tree branch. The wing looked dangerously fragile. The rivets holding its sections together seemed loose and jumpy, and it was all too easy to imagine the wind tearing it from the plane like the wing of a well-roasted chicken. Mortally crippled, the aircraft would surrender to gravity, plummeting toward certain destruction. I felt a shudder run up the length of my back. I shut the window shade firmly, click, plastic on plastic.

Leaning back against the headrest, I closed my eyes again and breathed in deeply. Between the breaths, among Eddie Jefferson's raspy falsetto notes, came the soft, husky alto of my mother's voice. "Blood is thicker than mud," she says, probably quite unaware that she's quoting Sly and the Family Stone, whose records I played almost incessantly for a couple of years in the early seventies. It's a family affair, indeed.

Clara was plenty bullish on family back when I was a kid. "When the chips are down, nobody wants you but your family," she'd say. And I think she really believed it. Of course, when my own personal chips were way, way down, the last people I could turn to were Clara and Lance. Lance last of all. But, I'm happy to say that I have since come to an uneasy peace with all that. For the most part.

"Boy, you just remember, these are your people." Lance's voice now, a tight, gruff hiss as he drags David and me to visit Lance's aunt Hattie, a slope-shouldered and surrealistically ugly woman, her misshapen face peppered with huge hairy moles and her head wrapped in a kerchief, Aunt Jemima–style; whose house had no indoor plumbing as late as the midsixties and smelled so rancid that I generally gagged immediately upon entry. And whose only child, Cousin Andrew, was a good five or six years older than I, but severely retarded, scooting along the sticky wood floors on all fours, usually clad in a perpetually dingy diaper and nothing else, drooling a slippery snail trail as he went, babbling secrets in a language known only to himself. Until recently, the most disturbing dreams I'd ever had starred my cousin Andrew.

Your people, Lance called his family. I must admit, I no longer consider my Louisiana relatives my "people" — in fact, I'd be hard pressed to think of any group of people I might consider mine (except maybe African-American queer musicians). But they were certainly Lance's people. The people he'd traveled hundreds of miles to be near when he died. And now that my father was wiping his big, flat feet on death's welcome mat, he had sent for me, his only surviving son, and I had reluctantly boarded this trembling craft to follow my father to the place he called Home, to his deathbed. After so many years. In spite of everything.

I swallowed dryly, like gulping down a fistful of dust, dragged a sandpapery tongue across my upper teeth, then clicked my tongue against the roof of my mouth as if speaking Swahili. It felt as if my salivary glands had ceased to function.

Ah, sweet marijuana.

I'd only smoked half a joint of old, not-so-hot weed I'd managed to mooch from my ex–piano player, scrunched down in the seat of my Corolla in the airport parking structure. But I've always been particularly susceptible to the effects, side effects, and aftereffects of drugs, any and all drugs. Which is why, except for Dramamine for travel across air, sea, or land, hay fever medicine for my chronic sinus problems, and not counting my recent romance with Xanax, I very seldom take drugs. Especially smoke — bad for the breath control, murder on the voice. Generally speaking, I only smoke anymore when I have to fly. A few hits of decent grass is usually just enough to keep me from going totally berserk at thirty thousand feet at the first threat of turbulence. And if it occasionally causes me mild aural hallucinations (like hearing my parents speaking, or Lady Day singing "I Cover the Waterfront" within the rumbling hum of the plane's engines), and if it never fails to make my mouth dryer than Prescott, Arizona, at high noon in mid-August, I have to consider it a fair trade.

I spotted the cute little blond flight attendant, What's-his-name, Barry Billy Benny, something — the one who'd recognized me shortly after takeoff, who'd tilted his head to one side and smiled and said, "You're Johnnie Ray Rousseau, aren't you? The singer?" — making his way up the aisle, and I flagged him down with a raised forefinger. I enjoyed a quick look at the crotch of the attendant's trousers (a lumpy, gold cotton-polyester-blend surprise package), before glancing upward.

The little plastic wings pinned to his blue-blazered chest said "Terry." I pulled out one earpiece, leaving Eddie Jefferson singing into my right ear alone, and said, "Terry, could I trouble you for another orange juice, please?" The attendant smiled something very similar to flirtation and said, "No trouble at all." I thanked Terry and returned his smile. Terry lobbed another one back over the net and punctuated it with a wink before he left. I replaced the left earpiece just as Eddie Jefferson sang "I'm through" and James Moody blew a flurry of heavenly sixteenth notes over the final fermata.

Ella kicked into "How High the Moon," and I thought, "I wonder if Terry's grinning and winking at me because he can tell I'm stoned?" A bit of mild, cannabis-induced paranoia. The dude was probably just flirting. The white boys have always liked me — what can I say? And even at my relatively advanced age of — well, thirty-something, I still get my share of looks. Thank heaven for Clara's Cherokee cheekbones and the entire line of Nautilus exercise machines.

Besides, the fact was, I was hardly buzzed at all. My shoulders were like clip-on earrings against the sides of my head and I couldn't seem to keep my fists unclenched for more than a few seconds at a stretch. I briefly considered taking a Xanax out of the travel bag stowed securely beneath the vacant window seat and washing it down with canned orange juice, but immediately thought better of it. They were for real emergencies, for calming the uncontrollable all-over shakes and seemingly endless sobbing jags the likes of which I hadn't experienced in well over three months. Taking a pill now would not only have been counter to my concerted effort to kick what as recently as four months before was just a scream away from a real live, genuine prescription drug addiction. It would also certainly have left me so groggy that, once we reached Lake Charles, cute little blond Terry would have to carry me from the plane like a 150-pound duffel bag.

I'd have sold my everlasting soul for a few tryptophane. Damn the FDA for pulling the blessed calming, sleep-encouraging amino acid off the market just because a few unfortunates seemed to have contracted a rare anemialike blood disease from some contaminated capsules. Tryptophane sleep had been deep as a warm well; tryptophane dreams had been sweet and sexy Cinerama head movies. And with no discernible side effects — not so much as dry mouth.

The jet plane suddenly shook and shimmied like a great metal cooch dancer. My entire body tensed at the first jolt, sweat began to gather clammy and pungent in my armpits and behind my knees, and fingers of nausea tickled my tummy from the inside, threatening to induce my special-order vegetarian lunch into an unscheduled comeback. "Breathe," I whispered, closing my eyes and drawing in a long, deep breath through my nose. I emptied my lungs slowly, imagining the tension flowing from my shoulders and thighs and hands, and leaving my body via my nostrils like car exhaust. Then filled my lungs again deeply, and out again slowly.

And deeply in.

And slowly, my fingers uncurled. My shoulders softened. And the plane steadied itself in the sky. And slowly out. And deeply in. Breathing. Breathing.

Breathing hard. My heart throbbing in my ears. Running down the long white hallway. Farther, farther. Ella scatting *oob-dee-oo-bee*, obviously Ella but strange and stretched, like an old, warped record album, like Muzak in hell, filling the hall, filling my head, vibrating through my chest cavity.

Running, running toward it, seeing it far at the end of the hallway.

Breathing hard. Standing at the gurney with the white, white sheet covering the body. Pushing into my chest with both palms, as if to keep my heart from tearing through my rib cage.

Trembling. Looking down, watching, unable to look away as the sheet peels itself down, down, slowly.

Trembling.

Keith's hair, stiff and matted. Keith's prominent brow, blackened and purple with bruises. Keith's eyelids, sunken and bluish. Someone screaming.

Screaming.

I was leaning forward from the waist, my legs tensed as if to jump, to run, to flee, something holding me back. Somebody was screaming and I suddenly realized it was me. I was screaming a long, continuous busy signal of a scream — *aah, aah, aah* — and I couldn't seem to make it stop.

I'd done this one before. But not in months. And never in a plane.

Something, somebody pushed me back by the shoulders, back into my seat. It wasn't until the voice called, "Sir? Sir?" that I realized my eyes were shut, and opened them up.

Boy — man — jacket — the flight attendant. Terry. Terry's small, strong hands gripped me by the shoulders, held me back against the headrest. Terry's face was close to mine, breathing through his mouth. His breath smelled minty, like chewing gum or Tic-Tacs. I noticed there was a little bit of gray in his hair at the temple and that his right earlobe was pierced. His eyes were opened wide, and (I suddenly noticed) nearly the same hazel as Keith's. "Are you all right?" he asked.

"I'm fine," I said between a couple chest-heaving breaths, lying to the flight attendant if not to myself. "I'm fine," I repeated, my hands around Terry's upper arms as if I might never release them.

"You sure?" Terry said.

"I'm fine," I said again, and just to say something different, I added, "Bad dream." I stared into Terry's eyes for a length of time I couldn't have begun to estimate, looking for God only knows what, until Terry twisted his torso a little, winced a little, and said, "You're hurting me."

"Oh God." My fingers sprang apart. "I'm sorry."

Terry smiled. "S'okay." He took my hands in his own and held them a moment. His hands were soft and warm. I wondered if I asked him nicely, might Terry agree to occupy my vacant window seat, gather me into his blue-blazered arms, and hold me, rock me the rest of the way to Lake Charles. Terry released my hands, leaving them feeling unaccountably cold. I rubbed my palms against my thighs, watching Terry, wishing he wouldn't leave.

"You relax," Terry said, giving my shoulder a little squeeze. "I'll get your juice." He lifted his hand from my shoulder, brushing his fingertips softly along my jawline before he turned away and started up the aisle.

It was then that I noticed the middle-aged white couple in the seats in front of me (he shiny bald on top, her hair dyed a uniform blonde which does not, to my knowledge, occur in nature) quickly turn away. Looking around to my left, I saw several others glance down into their coffees, their paperback novels, their *Newsweek* magazines. I heard the jazz leak from around my chest: my headset hung from my neck like high-tech jewelry. I reached for the Walkman still wedged between my thighs to switch off the music, then changed my mind and pulled the headset back over my head. Rickie Lee Jones was singing about a jukebox going "doyt-doyt."

I closed my eyes once again, leaned back against the headrest, and wondered, When do I get a break? When does it end?

There is no formal timetable for grief.

So Dennis had assured me just that morning. I'd scheduled an extra session, knowing how I'd need one, not knowing when the next one might be, visiting my therapist in lieu of breakfast.

"I just can't help feeling like I should be better by now," I'd said, pushed back into Dennis's big brown leather armchair, arms crossed tightly at the sternum — my usual posture during sessions with Dennis.

"How so?" Dennis made a little steeple with the forefingers of his pale, freckled hands, and arched one slender, copper-colored eyebrow. I looked at Dennis's smooth, snub-nosed face and shock of red hair, and wondered (as I so often wondered) how I could entrust my deepest feelings and thoughts, the slimiest creatures from the blackest lagoons of my soul, to a man who looked so much like Howdy Doody.

"How so," I repeated, like a parrot, and asked myself (as I do at some point during nearly every session) if therapy was doing me any good, if it would ever do me any good — or if I was just jerking off while helping

Dennis pay for his vacation home in Palm Springs. Finally, I said, "Have you ever seen *Auntie Mame?*"

Dennis raised both eyebrows this time. "Whom?"

"Auntie Mame," I said. "It's a movie. Nineteen fifty-something. Rosalind Russell. I can't believe you've never seen it." Amazing — a gay man who'd never seen *Auntie Mame.* Dennis shrugged. "Well," I said, "Roz Russell — she's Auntie Mame — her husband's dead, fell off a Swiss Alp on their honeymoon. And a year later, she's still in mourning, full-on ... mourning. Black dress, black veil, the whole ensemble." My throat went uncomfortably dry, and I swallowed around a little lump of soreness.

"Anyway," I said, "Auntie Mame's best friend, Vera — Coral Browne plays her, she was Vincent Price's wife—"

"In the movie?" Dennis asked.

"No," I said, my patience wearing a bit, "in real life. Anyway, she sees Roz Russell in full widow's weeds, head-to-toe black, and here her husband's been dead a whole year. And she gives Roz this very superior look — not unlike one of yours, Dennis." Dennis did another eyebrow raise, but did not respond. "And she says, 'Mame, Dahling, couldn't you have gone to purple by now?'" I picked at a piece of blue lint on the front of my best white LeCoste shirt, which piece of blue lint turned out to be a little spot of blue ink. "I used to think that was so funny," I said. I clenched my jaw for my most top-drawer upper-crust accent: "'Mame, Dahling, couldn't you have gone to purple by now?'"

The quote hung in the air a moment.

"And you think you should be in purple by now?" Dennis said in his typically even tone. I nodded, my throat closing rapidly, tears burning like ammonia in my eyes.

Dennis snatched a tissue from the ever-convenient box on his desk and held it toward me. He smiled his trademark little smile (corners of his lips curled slightly upward, no teeth showing), the smile that I find more and more frustratingly inscrutable as we go along, and said, "There is no formal timetable for grief."

"Yeah, right," I said aloud, then opened my eyes just in time to see the bald-headed man in the seat in front of me do a quarter turn from the neck, undoubtedly fearing another screaming jag from behind. I stretched my face into a wide-eyed, manic Lon-Chaney-as-the-Phantom-of-the-Opera grin. My neighbor's head spun forward. Rickie Lee was snappin' her fingers and rappin' about chicken in the pot, chicken in the pot, chicken in the pot...

It wasn't the heat — it was the humidity. Seconds after stepping off the 707 and onto the sun-softened tarmac, my entire body was coated with moisture, and a warm rivulet was beginning the long, tickling roll down the center of my back. Being in Lake Charles, Louisiana, in June was like sitting in the steam room at the Santa Monica Sports Connection with all your clothes on. I shifted my carryon from my right shoulder to my left and started toward the terminal. I hope Athena's waiting, I thought, taking a deep breath of warm, humid air through my nostrils. I could feel my sinuses click open behind my eyes: tropical air — Hawaii, the Caribbean, or south-western Louisiana — always made my sinuses happy.

Shifting the carryon again, I couldn't help wondering how much Athena had changed since I'd seen her last. I hadn't laid eyes on her in ten or eleven years, not since Grandma Mary's funeral. People changed. I had gotten used to running into people I hadn't seen in three or four months, at a party or the gym or at the health food store, and finding them utterly unrecognizable, actually looking at someone I'd known for years and saying, "Have we met?" But that's different, of course.

The most I could realistically expect a decade out of my sight to have wrought on the face and physique of my cousin Athena would be a subtle spreading of her hips and perhaps some gray in her hair. The women in my family tend to age very slowly.

I heard her before I saw her. Only a few steps into the tiny terminal (compared with L.A. International, it looked like a small branch library), I barely had time to register the feeling of blessed air-conditioning cooling my all-over leotard of sweat so fast it raised gooseflesh on my arms, before I heard the instantly familiar voice, a sweet, breathless mezzo-soprano — Athena always sounded as if she'd just been running, or maybe fucking. "Junie!" she called.

I felt my ears go warm and the hint of a lump at the back of my throat at the sound of this voice I'd known my whole life, calling out the name only my Louisiana relatives had used in over twenty years: my father's odd combo-diminutive of "Johnnie" and "Junior," the baby name that fell into immediate disuse around the Rousseau house once I entered the first grade, relegated to the upper shelf in the hall closet along with my old Raggedy Ann doll. Turning toward the sound of Athena's voice, I spotted her immediately, standing on tiptoe and waving an entire slender arm from the shoulder as if we were a football field apart instead of a few yards, smiling so big her light brown face seemed to be three-quarters teeth and gums. I matched that smile with one of my own as Athena stretched both her arms out toward me, tickling the air between us with her long fingers.

"Theenie," I said in greeting when I reached her. The first thing I noticed was her teeth: big and white and perfect, and somehow not exactly the smile I remembered from the last time I'd seen her. I placed my carryon gently onto the floor before allowing Athena to wrap her arms around my neck. "Junie, Junie, Junie," she said, as we held one another, rocking gently from side to side.

Athena felt small and delicate in my arms. Standing flat-footed, Athena in espadrilles and me in running shoes, both heads of hair natural and close cropped, we were almost exactly the same height; but I could feel the bones in Athena's back through her light blue, gauzy dress, one of those peasantish sack things with bright, primitive embroidery at the bodice that girls used to wear when I was in high school back in the seventies. I'd been wrong to expect any thickening of my cousin's figure: she seemed to have the chest and hips of a twelve-year-old boy.

She released her hold and stepped back. "Let me look at you," she said. "Ooh, child, you looking some kinda good," she said, smiling that smile. She squeezed my upper arms. "Lord, look at all these muscles on you, Junie!"

"God, Theenie," I said, simultaneously flattered and embarrassed. "Nobody calls me that anymore."

"No, I guess not. You mind?"

"Not from you," I said.

"Good," she said through another smile, "'cause I don't think I could make myself call you nothing else." Which is when it hit me: she'd had her teeth capped or crowned or something. Five or six years before, I'd heard through the family grapevine (via Clara) of Athena's dalliance with the Black Muslim faith and of the extreme vegetarian diet she'd adopted that left her sickly, skeletally thin, and calcium deficient, and her teeth gray and brittle. The perky-breasted, full-legged figure and high, wide smile that had helped make Athena second runner-up for Miss Black Louisiana back in '68 or '69 had been ruined by well-meaning malnutrition. Obviously, little of the lost weight had returned over the ensuing years, but at some point some bargain-basement dentist had equipped Athena with the sort of smile I've noticed only on black and Latina women of modest means: teeth too white, too even, and, to my eyes at least, too many.

"Nigel gonna go crazy for you," Athena said. "He's Mr. Weight Lifter all of a sudden. If he's not dropping them barbells on my floor, he's standing in the kitchen, drinking down raw eggs, like to make me sick."

A little chill ran up my back having nothing to do with the terminal's air-conditioning, and I made a quick mental note to counsel my young cousin on the dangers of salmonella poisoning. Nigel must be — what? — fifteen, sixteen years old by now, I thought. Or maybe more. Since the age of thirty, I've noticed time seems to smudge more and more, like a charcoal drawing. Off the top of my head, I couldn't remember the exact age difference between Athena's only son and myself; but my most recent memory of Nigel was of a small dark-chocolate child of maybe six. All elbows, kneecaps, and head, and the biggest, darkest eyes I'd ever seen on a boy so small. I recalled watching television in Aunt Lucille's big old calico-covered armchair, holding the boy in my lap; remembered the springy leanness of the boy's little body, and dirty Band-Aids covering scuffed, ashy knees.

Athena gestured toward my grounded carryon. "That all the luggage you brought?"

"This?" I picked up the bag and hung it over my shoulder. "Darlin', I pack heavier than this to go to the gym." I hooked my free arm around my cousin's slender shoulders and steered us toward the baggage carousel.

■

"Oh, my God." My face split into a smile as I followed Athena's narrow back toward the instantly familiar rear end of a sky blue 1966 Chevrolet Caprice sedan. "The

Blue Bomb!" I set down my suitcase and folded my
garment bag over my forearm as Athena shoved a key
into the trunk's lock and grunted quietly with the effort
of turning it. "I cannot believe you're still driving this
car," I said through a smile. Having broken a fresh
sweat during the fifty-odd-yard walk to the car, I
pushed a hand into my pants pocket, retrieved my
slightly damp handkerchief, and wiped it across my
sweat-dripping face.

"Believe it," said Athena, opening the great gaping
maw of a trunk. "Muh ain't never gettin' rid of this car,
and long as Nigel keep it running, why not drive it?" I
hoisted my luggage into the huge and amazingly clean
trunk and slammed the lid shut, the metal hot on my
fingers.

"God," I said, "I love this car." Originally my father's
car, the Caprice had carried my family from L.A. to
Louisiana and back again at least five times before
Lance tired of it and gave it to his sister Lucille as a
wedding gift for her fourth and final marriage. The
marriage had lasted less than a year, but the car was
obviously still running. Climbing into the passenger
seat, I smiled to myself, remembering when I'd had to
sit up tall to see over the car's blue vinyl dashboard. I
could almost feel my kid brother's little-boy muscle and
bone against my own as the two of us tussled in the
backseat, a backseat big enough to sleep both of us
comfortably until I was school-age. I could all but see
Lance's big hand and brawny, veiny arm swatting back
at us, hear his oft-repeated threats. "If I have to stop
this car," he'd shout through clenched teeth, "I'll whip
you 'til you can't sit down!" or "I'll bust yo' hides open!"
Which he'd actually done more than once: Lance's arm
and anger behind a thin leather belt were more than
capable of leaving an untidy cross-hatching of bloody
welts on little-boy legs.

"You wanna get high?" Athena pulled a slim silver-tone cigarette case from her voluminous fabric shoulder bag, flipped the case open, and removed a half-smoked hand-rolled cigarette.

"Thanks, no," I said.

"You don't smoke no more? Saving your voice, huh?" Athena struck a match against its box and lit the charred end of the roach, which popped and sparked.

"That's part of it," I said. "It's almost fifteen years since I've seen my dad. Now I've flown halfway across the country to come to his deathbed. Don't ask me why, but I think I'd rather be sober."

"Suit yourself," Athena said out of one side of her mouth, the roach parked in the other corner. She turned the ignition key, unleashing a muscular surge of horsepower and a welcome blast of frosty cool from the air-conditioning.

I felt the deep basso vibration of the big car beneath my thighs and haunches as Athena backed out of the parking space and headed out toward the road. "God," I said, leaning back against the seat, "this car's got serious balls." And we lit out toward St. Charles, the sleepy little excuse for a town just outside Lake Charles, which was hardly a teeming metropolis itself, known for little other than a mention in the song "Up on Cripple Creek" by the Band. It was the town where both my parents had been born, five years apart but within literal shouting distance of each other. Where my mother's seven-year-old thigh was sliced open by a nail protruding from a homemade seesaw, and the slapdash patch job done by the nearest doctor (a white man who only touched Clara's bleeding brown flesh at all because my maternal grandmother took in his family's laundry) left Clara with a discolored bas-relief scar the size of a Mont Blanc fountain pen, a scar she carries to this day. Where my father began work pulling

weeds in the rice fields at the age of nine. Where Clara
Jane Johnson and Lance Joseph Rousseau fell in love,
married, and then left as fast as a secondhand '50 Ford
could carry them.

Watching a long filmstrip of southwest Louisiana
blur by through the window, I noticed there seemed to
be considerably fewer low-hanging forests of poplar and
cottonwood, and considerably more strip malls and
video stores than the last time I'd had occasion to look.
I thought, The whole world is turning into Van Nuys.

"You want it?" Athena said.

"Do I want what?"

"This car," she said, as if several minutes hadn't
passed since I'd last mentioned the car. Sweet marijuana had obviously turned Athena's sense of time into
Silly Putty. "'Cause you should have it if you want it,
yeah."

I just shrugged. I've never been comfortable driving
big cars. Besides, trying to keep a land yacht like the
Bomb in gas in L.A. would probably break me. Also,
I'd have to drive the big tank all the way to Los
Angeles. And besides, it was all gloriously moot. "Dad
gave it to Aunt Lucille," I said. Another shrug. "It's
hers."

"Muh don't drive it. Don't drive a-tall no more,"
Athena said, tapping out the tiny butt in the ashtray.
She didn't say anything for a while, which was fine with
me, since it was silly of her to talk about giving away a
car she did not own.

I reached over and pointed the nearest air vent away
from my face (it was drying out my contact lenses) and
watched a little more Louisiana go by. Suddenly, Diana
Ross and the Supremes were singing "Love Child,"
Diana yodeling "I'll, always love, you-hoo-hoo." I hadn't
noticed before, but since the last time I'd ridden in the
Blue Bomb, someone had had an AM-FM stereo radio

and tape deck installed. I was about to mention it when Athena spoke.

"Junie, I was real sorry to hear about your friend."

I swallowed a little lump of residual sadness and another one made of equal parts frustration, impatience, and anger; then said, "Thank you." I hoped she'd let it drop. I didn't feel like talking about all that right then, didn't feel like dealing with all that right then, not so close to having to deal with Lance, and me hundreds of miles from my analyst.

A long moment passed (long enough for "Love Child" to end and "Someday We'll Be Together" to begin) before Athena said, "You all right?"

I closed my eyes, took in a long breath, and let it out. "Sure," I said.

"Rilly?"

I've always liked Athena's odd pronunciation of the word "really." Rilly, she said. I very nearly smiled before admitting, "Hell, no." I turned back to the window. Slowly, oh so slowly, I realized I could feel each and every individual fiber of my shirt against my skin, feel every drop of sweat on my forehead, feel every one of my hair roots planted in my scalp. Diana Ross seemed to be singing from somewhere near the center of my chest. I was obviously coming onto one lulu of a contact high.

I felt Athena's hand, small and warm on my own. Her voice was like a backup vocal on the tape, mixed way back.

"Poor Junie," she said, stroking my hand.

 **3.** If I'd been stone blind, I'd have known exactly when we entered St. Charles, by the smell of it coming through the air-conditioning vents. The town possessed a scent all its own, an aroma I have yet to smell anywhere else I've ever been: the thick, dark, fertile smell of perpetually moist reddish claylike soil; the acrid stench of the shipyard at Lake Charles that supplied most of the jobs in the area and which rendered the local tap water unsuitable for drinking; the occasional farm animal, damp fur and droppings; the outhouses many of the elder locals continued to use in spite of the thirty-odd-year-old predominance of indoor plumbing; some-body's big, steaming pot of chitlins; and God only knows what else.

The smell of St. Charles had not changed since I'd last taken it into my lungs, Lord, so many years before. Little else seemed to have changed, either. Unlike the surrounding area we'd just passed through, which seemed to be undergoing an inevitable transformation into some sort of generic Small American Town, Early 1990s model, St. Charles looked like the land that time forgot. The Caprice's tires crunched against the road leading to my aunt Lucille's house, a dirt road paved only with a layer of tiny pieces of seashell, an anachronistically primitive road given over to mud slicks and potholes big enough to suck up a Volkswagen, with no sidewalks, no curbs. Just as it had been when I was a small child — as it likely had been when my father was a child.

Athena slowed and pulled the Caprice over to the side of the road next to the familiar old house. The big, rambling one-story wood-frame house my aunt Lucille shared with her daughter and grandson hadn't changed much, either. Perhaps it hadn't been painted since I'd seen it last, or maybe it had been rewashed Pepto Bismol pink with paint left over from the previous job. Like most of the houses in that flood-prone area, it was built two or three feet up off the ground on concrete blocks, with a flat, corrugated aluminum roof that sounded like a one-note steel band when the rain came down, and a big, wooden porch to one side, securely screened in to let in the relative cool of an evening while keeping out the battalions of mosquitoes that invariably arrived with the dusk.

I noticed the dilapidated waist-high wire fence I remembered had been replaced by new chain link, and the homemade lean-to of a garage was gone, a new one (sturdy-looking and painted the same color as the house) in its place.

"I thought we were going directly to the hospital," I said as Athena arm-wrestled the car into Park.

"No, baby," Athena said, shoving open her door and climbing out. "I got an appointment. Miss Emma Louise — you remember Miss Emma Louise, was married to Uncle Pepper, had that tumor removed a year ago Christmastime — she suddenly decided she got to have her hair pressed and curled and can't nobody do it but me. Don't want Muh's hands near her old nappy head."

I got out of the car, felt the oppressive damp heat envelop me. Athena was struggling with the trunk's lock, which turned with a metallic pop as I approached.

"Nigel take you over to the hospital," Athena said, draping my garment bag over one slender arm.

Aunt Lucille was standing in the doorway behind the screen door as I followed Athena across the little wooden footbridge built across the three-foot-deep storm ditch that either David or I or both of us inevitably fell into at least once every visit here when we were children. I walked down the wobbly walkway (old bricks set into the muddy earth) toward the house, starting at the sound of a dragonfly humming a post-bop solo into my ear, moving none too quickly due to luggage, heat, Dramamine, and a slight marijuana buzz.

"Junie!" Aunt Lucille called, leaning to one side to peer around her daughter. "How you doin', cher?" ("Cher" is French for "dear" and is pronounced "sheh" by Louisiana Cajuns and Creoles such as my aunt Lucille). Then, to Athena, "Girl, you better get on in there. Emma Louise been here twenty minutes, trying to eat *all* my tea cakes."

"I'll put this in the back room," said Athena, indicating the garment bag she carried, then quickened her step and rushed past her mother into the house.

Like her house, like her town, Lucille Thibodeaux had barely changed in more than a decade. Her smooth, light brown face was nearly as unlined as Athena's. Her hair had been dyed and straightened and chemically and mechanically influenced into a snug-fitting cap of stiff, rust-colored curls, as it had been for as long as I could remember. The soft curves of her breast-heavy, broad-hipped body (Lucille's figure always made me think of that line from *South Pacific* about being "broad where a broad should be broad") were draped with one of her many caftans, this one of a bright, vaguely

African pattern. Though she was hardly the wraith Athena was, Lucille was not a fat woman, only full figured: she wore flowing, loose garments simply because she found them comfortable. This was also the rationale behind the bedroom slippers which barely contained her wide feet, and which she always wore unless planning to leave the house, which, to my knowledge, she seldom did.

"Lord, you sure looking good, cher," Aunt Lucille said, wrapping me up in a hug, surrounding me in her arms, her caftan, and her sweet bodily scents. An inveterate cook and baker as far back as I can recall, Aunt Lucille had always smelled vaguely edible, her hands never far from a flour-covered breadboard, patting out piecrusts with her fingers — she never used a rolling pin — or cutting out tea cakes with a drinking glass, her body lightly dusted with flour, sugar, and cinnamon. As a child, I often imagined one could eat Aunt Lucille herself, bit by bit like a gingerbread man. Now, her wonted bakery smells were undercut by the scents of various shampoos, pomades, curl activators, and singed hair.

"Give y'old aunt Lucille some sugar," she said, raising herself slightly on tiptoe to receive my kiss on her silky cheek. Taking my face in her plump, soft, sweet-smelling hands (with at least one flashy but inexpensive ring adorning each finger), she looked up into my eyes with the gentle smile of one who considers hardship, physical or emotional, to be proof that one is among God's chosen, and said, "You poor little baby. Never rains but when it pours." She dropped her vocal volume a bit to add, "I was real sorry to hear about your friend."

I felt myself stiffen, hoped Aunt Lucille didn't notice. I glanced over my aunt's shoulder at the pictorial triptych hanging over the television set: a formal photograph of John F. Kennedy, a brightly colored print of Jesus Christ (nimbus adorning simple, center-parted coif and big, puppy dog eyes lifted heavenward), and a photo of the Reverend Dr. Martin Luther King, Jr., mouth open and hand upraised, presumably delivering the "I have a dream" speech. I managed a "Thank you."

"You hungry, baby?" she asked, lowering her hands. "Why don't I get Nigel to put your bags in the back room and I'll fix you some food."

"Thank you, ma'am," I said. "I'm not hungry." There was still something about coming back to this place that made me automatically start "sir"- and "ma'am"-ing my elders, very Elvis Presley.

"Got some good boudin in the icebox. I know you can eat you some boudin." Boudin, pronounced "BOO-dan," is a concoction of spicy rice seasoned with peppers and giblets or ground beef, stuffed into sausage casing, and consumed in mass quantities, hot or cold. Serious good eatin', people.

Aunt Lucille had always seemed to be of the heartfelt belief that earth had no sorrow that good food, prepared with generous amounts of garlic, black pepper, chopped onions, and love, could not heal. Or at least anesthetize temporarily, like Bactine. I would not have been surprised to learn that she had attempted to send my father's cancer into remission using megadoses of her seafood-okra gumbo — which, according to local reports, has in fact given eyesight to the blind.

"Thank you, ma'am," I said, "but not just yet. I was kind of hoping to get to the hospital to see Dad."

Something — a thought, a worry, something — seemed to move across Aunt Lucille's face, briefly crimping her smooth brow. She blinked it quickly away and said, "All right, cher. Lemme get Nigel in here to he'p you with your bags. He'll drive you over to the hospital." She leaned into the doorway leading to the big room used as both a guest room and sewing room, with two twin beds against opposite walls, two fully functional sewing machines, various supplies, and garments in varying states of completion.

"Nigel!" she called. "Come see your cousin Junie!" Quietly, to me, she added, "Probably got that Walkman thing wrapped around his long head." I had to stifle a laugh, Walkman junkie that I am. Aunt Lucille punched both fists into her hips and called again, louder: "Nigel!"

From the far end of the house came the tenor-voiced reply: "Ma'am?"

Through the doorway, I watched him round the corner into the sewing room, slender and chocolaty brown, barefoot and shirtless.

"Queenie," he said, a teenage whine in his voice, "I was just fixin' to—" We made eye contact and he stopped. A wide, white, slightly crooked smile spread across the boy's face. "Captain!" he said, striding his way toward me, long-fingered right hand outstretched. "Long time."

I accepted Nigel's hand, finding his palm cool and smooth, his grip firm. The boy's eyes met mine again, briefly, then seemed to take in the rest of me like twin video cameras. Watching Nigel's eyes flicker up and down my face and body, I could feel my cheeks go hot, as if my pants had fallen down in a public place.

Releasing my hand, Nigel said, "You're looking good, Captain. Real good."

My voice sounded strange to my own ears as I said, "You too, kid. You've really—"

I quickly scanned Nigel's naked torso: he wasn't much for muscle mass, but his weight lifting had obviously brought some results, judging from the muscular delineation of the boy's flat belly and chest. His nipples protruded from that chest like Hershey's Kisses. My mind immediately served up a picture of myself taking one of those nipples into my mouth, and in an attempt to escape the little mental porno flick, I glanced downward, where my eyes encountered a lump in the crotch of Nigel's blue jeans that brought a second hot flush to my face. I glanced about the room in search of something else to focus on. Looking past Nigel's bare shoulder at an indeterminate point somewhere in the sewing room, I swallowed dryly and rasped, "You've really grown." The last time I'd seen my cousin, he'd barely reached my hip. Now he was looking me dead in the eye — not that I'm tall, heaven knows — but suddenly here he was, a full-grown young man. With a full-grown basket.

"Little fart be nineteen in fo' months," said Aunt Lucille, giving Nigel a playful cuff upside the head. My cousin's hair had been cut so short as to look painted on, a long part etched in scalp-deep on the left side.

"Queenie," Nigel said, doing an exaggerated recoil from his grandmother's hand, "don't be messing with my do, now."

"I'll be messing with more than your do, you don't help your cousin take his bags in the back."

A little smile on his lips, Nigel looked directly into my face and said, "His arms twice as big as mine. He can carry his own bags."

"What you say, boy?" Aunt Lucille raised a threatening, be-ringed hand.

Nigel stepped back, laughing. "Just funnin', Queenie," he said, lifting my suitcase from the floor.

"I'll kick your raggedy butt 'til your nose bleed," said Aunt Lucille, a chuckle in her voice betraying her amusement, "silly ol', big-headed boy. You think you can stop acting a fool long enough to put on some clothes and drive your cousin to the hospital to see his daddy?"

"Yes, ma'am," Nigel said through a naughty-boy grin that was beginning to add to the already considerable dampness in the crotch of my pants.

"Then get on out of my face, then! I got to get back to my customer." Aunt Lucille palmed my face with one fragrant hand and said, "Junie, come see me before you go. I'll be out in the shop, pressing what's left of Annie Mae Leopold's hair." And she started off through the kitchen.

"Follow me, Captain Cuz," Nigel called as he carried my case away.

Watching Nigel's wide-shouldered, tiny-waisted, oh-so-bare back walking away, taking a high-set blue denim butt along for the ride, I sucked in a deep, long yoga breath and blew it out. "He's your cousin," I told myself. "He's your little baby cousin."

4.

"Pardon me, Captain." Nigel reached his arm across me and flipped open the Caprice's glove compartment. From an armpit left bare by the baggy-fitting red tank top Nigel had pulled on, I caught the pungent, rather heady odor of humid black boy mixed with Mennen Speed Stick deodorant (which I myself had used for a while before settling into my present habit of a splash of Old Spice after-shave under each arm). Nigel fingered around the various objects in the glove box — some pens and pencils, papers of some kind, some loose cassette tapes, and some empty cassette tape boxes — and retrieved a labeled but boxless tape. With the same hand, he ejected the tape in the player, tossed it into the glove box and shut it, then pushed his tape into the machine. As he turned the ignition key, the sounds of internal combustion were overpowered by the sound of a jackhammer backbeat and the in-your-face aggressive rhyming shout of a rapper. I cringed involuntarily from the musical assault.

"Not a big NWA fan, Cap?" Nigel shouted over the din.

"Can't say that I am," I shouted back, pushed as far back into the seat as my leg muscles could accomplish. In fact, I considered most rap infantile, puerile doggerel requiring little or no musical talent. This opinion was no doubt colored by a certain amount of professional jealousy, since I had never made more than go-out-to-dinner money as a singer, while teenage boys shouting over rhythm tracks of records I danced to in high school raked in zillions of dollars. And, I considered the rap group Niggers with Attitude particularly distasteful on the strength of its name alone.

"No sweat, Captain," Nigel said, lowering the volume. He pressed the automatic reverse button and NWA instantly gave way to Sarah Vaughan. "Just friends," crooned the familiar thick, slurry contralto over gentle swing accompaniment, "lovers no more."

"You like?" Nigel did that naughty smile again. It seemed to be chronic.

"Yes," I admitted. "Thanks."

"Anything for you, Captain," Nigel said, shoving the car into Drive and starting us down the road, sending tiny bits of seashell clattering in our wake.

"And what exactly is this 'Captain' thing?" I asked, watching my cousin's fine-boned profile. Nigel flashed a quick smile in my general direction, then faced the windshield again.

"Just something I say sometimes," Nigel replied with a little shrug of his shoulders. "Lester Young called everybody 'Lady' — I call people 'Captain.' Except for Muh. And Queenie, she's always Queenie."

"Lester Young?" I said as Nigel braked for a stop sign.

"Tenor sax," Nigel said, checking both sides of the intersection before continuing through the stop. "Maybe the greatest. They called him 'Prez.' He was the first to call Billie Holiday 'Lady Day.'"

"I know who he was," I said, turning in the seat toward Nigel. "The big surprise here is that you know from Prez." Indicating the tape player, I added, "And

Sarah. You know about this and you can still listen to..." I made a shit-smelling face coupled with a finger-wiggling hand gesture.

Nigel laughed, a little low chuckle from somewhere in his belly. "So Captain Cuz don't think this town is big enough for Sarah Vaughan and Niggers with Attitude?"

"In a word, no," I said.

"Tut-tut, Captain," Nigel said, giving me a playful pinch on the nearest shoulder, causing my face to split into the closest thing to a full-fledged grin I could remember in quite some time. "Just tut-tut."

Sarah was four or five bars shy of the coda of "Just Friends" before Nigel said, "We're here," and pulled the car toward the curb in front of the hospital.

I peered out the window at the three-story box of a building, at the brushed-chrome identifying lettering attached to its granite face, and felt the lead balloon inflate in my guts, bringing the familiar gaseous over-full feeling that always accompanies nervousness, apprehension, dread. It had been nearly a decade and a half since I'd last seen my father, and the circumstances of that last encounter were such that I would have felt the lead balloon even if I were meeting Lance for lunch at the Polo Lounge at the Beverly Hills Hotel, let alone sidling up to his bedside in the intensive care unit at St. Charles Hospital.

Among the images I am quite certain I will carry with me to the grave is that of my father's movie-star-handsome face twisted into hateful ugliness as he called me faggot.

"I don't know what I could've done to make the good Lord punish me like this," he'd said. "Lose my one real son, and this is what I got left. A god-damn faggot."

The horror my parents and I had shared from the death of my brother David — one of seven victims of a random drive-by shooting in front of a Westwood Village movie theater — had been less than six months old when I, dopey on the drug of new love, had made the mistake of bringing my then-lover on a visit to my parents' home, igniting an explosion of righteous disgust from my father. My sexuality had been the unspeakable subject in Lance's house since he and Clara had been made aware of it during my senior year in high school. The appearance of my white male lover was more than Lance had been willing to abide.

"Take your ... boyfriend," Lance said through a sneer, "and get out of my house." He jabbed a blunt index finger at my face. "Now. Before I put a hurt on you you won't ever forget."

"Lance, please." Clara settled a calming hand on her husband's shoulder, but he slapped it away. "Shut up," he snapped. "That's his whole problem. Mama's boy. Get the hell out of my house, mama's boy," he said, turning his face away, dismissing me, his only surviving son, with an arm motion like the swatting of a fly. "Don't come back."

"Lance," Clara said quietly as I started for the door, "you don't mean that. He's your son."

"I got no sons," my father replied. "My son is dead."

"Yo, Captain," Nigel said, waving a hand back and forth in front of my face, bringing me out of my unpleasant reverie. "I said we're here."

The lead balloon shifted up toward my throat as I entered the hospital's automatic doors and encountered the universally pervasive hospital smell of alcohol and illness, disinfectant and death. I didn't realize I'd stopped walking until I felt Nigel's hand on my shoulder, directing me toward the reception desk. "C'mon, Cap," he said softly.

A plain-looking twenty-something black woman in a crisp white uniform looked up from some paperwork as we approached the desk. Beaded braids hung from beneath her nurse's cap.

"L.J. Rousseau, please," Nigel said.

"You blood-related?" the woman asked.

"This is his son," Nigel said. I nodded dumbly, suddenly doubly grateful for Nigel's presence: it would likely have taken me several minutes to express any coherent thought to the sour-looking young nurse, and without Nigel to prod me along, I was none too sure I could have made myself move. The nurse began giving directions, but Nigel said, "I know the way."

Nigel led me with gentle fingers against my shoulder, as if I were Ray Charles. He summoned the elevator, entered first, and pressed the button for the third floor. When the doors opened, I lifted first one, then the other leaden foot out of the elevator, but couldn't seem to move any farther forward. I felt the trembling begin in my knees and thigh muscles, and within a second or two I was shivering like a naked man in a blizzard. "Yo," Nigel said, applying his hands, warm and strong, to my shoulders, "Captain."

I tried to speak, but only got as far as "I — I—"

Nigel slipped his arms around my shoulders and held me. "Easy, Cap," he said softly into my ear. "Easy."

It lasted less than a minute, and then the trembling stopped as quickly as it had begun, leaving me feeling more than a little foolish. "I'm all right," I said, just a bit too loud.

"You sure?" Nigel asked, releasing my shoulders, lowering his arms. I nodded, my voice deserting me for the moment. Nigel stepped around to face me. "Did Queenie talk to you?" he asked. "Tell you what to expect?"

I nodded again, and managed to say, "Yes."

"You won't hardly recognize him," Aunt Lucille had said, talking to me while concentrating on the head of hair and burning-hot straightening comb beneath her fingers.

I'd stood leaning against the wall of the little one-room hair salon Aunt Lucille and Athena ran behind the house, my nose turned up at the harsh scents of chemicals and singed hair, and said, "I've seen sick people before, ma'am."

"I don't believe you've seen this kind of sick," Aunt Lucille insisted.

I stifled a bitter little laugh. How sheltered she was. It really never occurred to her how many hospital rooms I'd seen over the past five, ten years. How many friends I'd watched die slowly, slowly, and then suddenly in fast-forward. I fought back the urge to count the ways in which I had seen "that kind of sick," loudly and with gestures.

I wanted to name names:

I wanted to tell her about Crockett Miller, my friend, confidant, and off-again-on-again sometimes fuck-buddy; blond and green-eyed with a tightly muscled, well-packed ex-college-gymnast's physique, a high-set, gravity-defying *tuchus* the likes of which comes once (maybe twice) in any given generation, and a weakness for Bruce Springsteen records and my recipe for lasagna with meat sauce; whom AIDS reduced to a sixty-some-odd-pound skeleton with skin before finally finishing him off at the age of thirty-two.

I could have told her about John Calhoun, a sweet Southern stud with whom I shared a word-processing center at a small Beverly Hills real estate syndication firm for about nine months and who shared his disheveled brass bed with me on more than one occasion during that time and after; and whose warm, sexy personality helped chip away at my old knee-jerk prejudice against all Southern white men (which equated a Dixie accent with ignorance, bigotry, bed sheets worn as clothing, and the *N* word); a ballet dancer turned bodybuilder whom I prefer to remember as a handsome, healthy man with a truly amazing set of pecs topped off with a truly amazing set of nipples, and for the sound of his velvety Georgia drawl when he called me "Dawlin'" and "Shuggah" (but never, not even once, the *N* word); but who haunts my nighttime dreams and waking memories as a sad, saddening being, propped up in a hospital bed, puffy beyond recognition with retained fluids, and breathing with great difficulty through plastic tubing, his once-magnificent body decimated, his formerly kitten-quick mind scrambled with HIV-induced dementia, conversation all but impossible as the doors and windows of his brain one by one closed tight on the words for simple everyday objects like "cup."

Or Marc Sloane, aspiring screenwriter, aspiring actor, aspiring painter of quasi-impressionist canvases, whose smooth mahogany skin was laid to ruin first by great craterlike shingles lesions, later with Kaposi's sarcoma lesions. And who, up to the last, continued to run on about "The Cure." As in, "If I can keep my T-cells up, I'll be a much better candidate for The Cure." And, "I've got to try to hang on until The Cure." And whose parents shipped his wasted corpse to Pittsburgh (where they resided and where Marc had been born), for a closed-casket memorial service which pointedly excluded those — myself included — who had cooked his meals and cleaned his apartment when he was too weak to do it himself and far too broke to hire someone to do it; who read to him and sang to him and held his woefully enfeebled hand in the hospital; and who later gathered around photographs of Marc taken during better days for a service of our own.

All that beauty and more, all that talent and more, gone gone gone, bye-bye, baby, and amen, struck down in the relative youth of late twenties and thirty-some-thing by an elusive, ever-mutating viral horror movie that doesn't just kill you dead, but kills you *ugly*.

I wanted to point out that there were other ways to die that were as horrible to behold as pancreatic cancer, and that in my time I'd personally seen some. Oh, not as many as some I know — those who have lost twenty, thirty friends, who have thrown away entire address books full of friends, lovers, and acquaintances, who have cried until there are no tears left, and who still, amazingly, keep going, keep caring, keep loving.

But I let it go, and said nothing. Maybe another time, but not right then, not with my dear aunt's hands full of hot comb and hair, and my father waiting for me in some hospital bed. I saw no reason to go into it with Nigel either, who no doubt saw me as a whimpering, weak-kneed crybaby and probably wasn't far wrong.

"He's in that room there," Nigel said, indicating the open doorway just to my left. "Want me to go in with you?"

I said, "No," and started toward the door, then added, "Thank you."

"Anything for you, Cap," Nigel said, almost a whisper.

The tiny room was filled to near capacity with equipment I could not have begun to identify: shiny metal giants with harsh video-screen faces. As many bedside visits as I'd made over the past several years, I had never absorbed the names or functions of the various pieces of apparatus that both dominated and documented the lives of the mortally ill, these glass-and-metal roommates I had seen so many times before. I recognized the line of light hopping across one screen as some sort of monitor of the patient's heart rate, but I'm pretty sure I knew that from television, "Marcus Welby," that sort of thing.

I looked toward the bed and immediately decided I must have stepped into the wrong room. One look at the frail little old man lying on the bed near the center of the claustrophobically small room, barely seeming to make a dent in the mattress, and I was sure I had walked in on some unfortunate stranger. I turned to leave — Nigel had obviously made a mistake, or maybe I had misunderstood — but then I turned and looked again. I took one, then another step toward the bed, toward the old man who lay there asleep (or perhaps just resting), his body in that odd hospital-bed position, his head raised well above parallel to the bed. The nose piece from a tank of oxygen reached into his nostrils and an IV protruded from the center of one of the long bony arms lying at his either side, palms up, like a saint displaying stigmata.

"Oh my God," I said aloud, and walked slowly around one side of the bed, finally able to see in this skeletally thin, white-haired man, the remains of my once imposingly robust father. I stood staring into my father's face — once so handsome he had more than once been mistaken for Harry Belafonte, now sunken into itself, looking twenty years older than Lance's sixty-two years. Lance's skin looked strangely dark, as if he'd been sunburned. His breath whistled softly around the nose piece, like the wind through the attic of an old house. His lips were closed tightly on one side, slightly parted on the other, revealing a sharp canine tooth. It reminded me of the face of a dog killed on the freeway.

I realized my hands were pressed one atop the other against my collarbone, a Lillian Gish gesture that left me slightly embarrassed, despite the fact that no one saw me. I lowered my arms quickly and rested my fingers along the bed's safety rail. Unable to tell if my father was asleep, resting his eyes, or in some sort of narcotic stupor, I stood for several long, uncomfortable moments tapping my fingertips softly against the bed-rail, trying to decide whether to attempt to rouse Lance or to tiptoe away and return later. Suddenly, Lance's sunken eyelids fluttered, then opened. My breath caught, and I jumped back a step.

"Dad," I said in a hushed voice.

Lance's pale, green-brown eyes moved rapidly right and left, then opened wide. "David?" he said, turning his head with what seemed like some difficulty toward my voice. I felt a little lead fist slug me hard in the belly.

"No, Dad," I said, moving in close to the bed. "It's me. Johnnie."

Lance's head pivoted away, facing forward.

"What are you doing here?" Lance said. It sounded less like a question than an accusation. His voice was a rough, gritty sound, like gravel under your shoe; the chesty resonance I remembered was gone.

"You sent for me," I said slowly. Was it a by-product of disease and medication that my father was now given to memory lapses?

"Like hell," Lance said, grinding the gravel a little harder. "Get out of here," he added, closing his eyes. "Go home."

"What are you talking about?" I protested. "You asked me to come." My own voice sounded shrill and desperate to my ears, as it so often had when I spoke with my father. "Aunt Lucille—" Suddenly, it was as if I'd been taken by the shoulders and shaken hard. I looked at my father's concave face, his eyes closed, his entire face closed. I made no good-byes as I left the room: I had already been dismissed.

I walked to the elevator on shaking legs and slapped at the Down button. I saw Nigel over in the waiting area put down a magazine and rise quickly from his chair and hurry toward me. I was trembling again, all over.

The emotion had changed but not the physical manifestation. I attempted to steady myself with a palm pressed flat against the wall.

"Yo, Captain," Nigel said as he approached. He started to extend a hand toward me, then pulled it back.

"Let's go," I said.

"You look like you better sit down, Cap," Nigel said, reaching out again and this time resting a hand on my shoulder.

"Let's go," I repeated. The elevator rang its arrival and I stepped inside, followed by Nigel. I leaned hard against the handrail, gripping it so tight with my hands its edges seemed to cut into my palms.

■

From the day my brother was killed until the day my mother divorced my father and received the family home in the settlement, David's bedroom was left exactly as it was the afternoon he departed the house for Westwood in his best friend Brian Lucas's father's AMC Pacer. His Nerf basketball hoop remained clipped to the top of the door, his Kareem Abdul Jabbar posters Scotch-taped to the walls, his Tower of Power albums on the floor, far from their respective covers — a shrine to a fallen hero.

After what she considered a reasonable period of mourning — I recall it was at least a year — Clara suggested one evening that perhaps it might be time to clear David's room. And make no mistake about it, Clara mourned her second son. She cried at David's funeral like nothing I'd ever seen before, her petite body convulsed with sobbing, beastly growls and gurgles erupting from her throat. She waved bye-bye toward my brother's coffin, repeatedly calling, "Bye, baby," in a heartbreaking singsong. Lance sat to one side of her, straight-backed and stone-faced as Michelangelo's Moses, silent as the tears that coursed down a face that had not known sleep in several nights.

Clara knocked on David's bedroom door every morning for a week after his death, to wake him for summer school. And fell to weeping again each time. I joined her in the doorway and cried with her more than once, rocking my mother's small-boned body in my arms as we shared our grief.

Dennis has accused me of experiencing David's death only as it affected my relationship with Lance.

That's just not true: I loved my brother. And his ridiculous, senseless, premature death pained me. Pains me.

I envied David, of course. Envied him his fair-skinned, green-eyed good looks, his athletic prowess, his indisputable position as our father's favorite. And who could blame me if it was my habit to dwell upon that aspect of my relationship with my brother as I sat back in Dennis's big armchair, spewing forth all my trials? Rather than regaling him with stories of David and me making jumpsuits for troll dolls out of old felt and buttons and Elmer's glue, or David and me convulsing one another with flawless imitations of Brother This and Sister That from the First New Ship of Zion Missionary Baptist Church, or David and me singing and acting out the rock opera *Jesus Christ Superstar* in its entirety (including scat-singing the totally instrumental "39 Lashes"), unaccompanied, in my room on a rainy day? Who could really blame me for leaving all that out? I mean, who goes to the analyst to talk about *nice* things? The things that still make me smile and sting my eyes when I remember them.

I mourned my brother, thank you very much — nearly as much (I'd imagine) as my mother did. But nobody mourned David like Lance. He repeatedly called me by my brother's name, looked right at me and said, "David, would you—," "David, I—" And his disappointment upon realizing again and again that David was gone and only I was left was a thing unto itself, an object almost, something I could feel covering me like an unwanted blanket on a hot night. He took to carrying some object or another of David's around with him — an old baseball, one of his swimming trophies — turning the thing around in his hands, touching it to his cheek as he sat slouched in front of the television.

And when, over a year after David's death, Clara dared to propose to her husband that David's old room be converted into a guest room, a sewing room, anything — Lance, without averting his gaze from Tom Brokaw and the evening news, said, "No."

"But, Lance," she attempted.

"I said no." And that was the end of it.

■

No words passed between us until Nigel had driven a block or two from the hospital. Sarah Vaughan was finishing up "Just Friends" with a high scat flourish. "You want to stop somewhere?" Nigel asked. "Have a beer or something? Talk?"

My body no longer shivered as if palsied. I trembled only on the inside. "No," I said slowly and carefully, "thank you."

Nigel suddenly pulled the car over and parked, for no reason I could discern, in front of a Winn-Dixie supermarket. (I suddenly remembered an old television commercial from my later childhood, where a crew-cut young white man sang, "Now aren't you glad you're shoppin' at Winn-Dixie?" to a store full of grinning, strutting, obviously glad white people.)

"Listen, Captain," Nigel said, turning his body toward me, "I know what you think: What could this dumb-ass kid know? Okay, maybe I'm a kid," he said, nodding his head up and down. "But I'm not dumb. I know you've been through a lot of serious shit."

I stared out the windshield: a skinny white teenager with a bad complexion was helping a fat white lady in too-tight white pants carry her groceries from Winn-Dixie's door to her car. I didn't want to talk to my cousin at that moment, and I certainly didn't want to listen to him. I wanted to go back to my sweetly scented caftan-clad aunt and treat her to a tongue-lashing the memory of which she would carry to the crypt.

"I know you must be hurtin'," Nigel continued, "seeing your daddy like he is now. And after what happened to your friend—"

"He was not my friend!" I snapped, turning to face Nigel. "He was my lover. He was my fucking husband, okay? He was my—" I searched the car's ceiling for that phrase of Paul Monette's. Oh, yes. "He was," I said, enunciating each word carefully, "the core of my heart." I snorted some snot, making an ugly wet noise. I realized I was crying. I looked away, feeling utterly ridiculous, shoved fingers into my pocket, digging for my handkerchief — not an easy task from a seated position. I raised the left side of my ass and straightened my leg as best I could, finally tugging the already damp handkerchief free. I blotted my eyes and blew my nose, honking like a goose in flight.

"Feel better now?" Nigel said softly.

Not yet facing Nigel, I said, "Little bit."

"I knew that," Nigel said after a moment. "I knew he was your lover." Exaggerating the pronunciation of each word in a parody of a Southern politician or maybe a Baptist preacher, he added, "I was employing a euphemism."

I let out a long breath, phlegm rattling at the back of my throat. How could I explain to this boy how it felt to be considered less than good, less than healthy, less than godly, often less than lawful in the eyes of society at large, simply because of whom you love? When simply to take your lover's hand in a public place can be considered "flaunting your sexuality," not quite in good taste; when that act in itself, or even just being seen entering or leaving a particular bar or dance club, might be sufficient provocation for some to attack, to inflict injury with bats and rocks and broken glass? How to explain to a nearly nineteen-year-old country cousin how it felt to have the great love of your life constantly referred to as "your friend"? Or how hurtful and offensive a well-meaning euphemism could become once Fate or Karma or the Lord who giveth and who taketh away has ripped that loved one from your life, leaving a hollowed-out, shivering, nightmare-haunted wreck where a relatively well-adjusted, functional person once sat?

You don't explain it, I decided. "I'm sorry," I said finally, sitting up, still not looking at Nigel. "I had no right to take this out on you."

"Never mind," said Nigel, turning the ignition key. "Just never you mind."

■

The Caprice had barely come to a complete stop in front of Aunt Lucille's house before I was out of the car, half jogging through the gate and toward the front door, propelled by the last dregs of my anger and hurt. "Aunt Lucille," I called as I crossed the living room, and again ("Lu-CILLE!," long and high, like Little Richard in concert), marching through the kitchen and out the back door, down the wooden stairs and into the marshy backyard. My shoes made wet squishy noise against the moist grassy ground as I headed for the beauty shop.

Through the screen door, I could hear the Swan Silvertones singing creamy harmony — "Oh, Mary, don't you weep; oh, Martha don't you moan." I could see Aunt Lucille turn toward the sound of my footsteps against the wooden stairs. I swung the door open wide and stepped in like John Wayne through the swinging saloon doors, fire irons at the ready, prepared for a showdown. The screen door swung shut with a loud *ka-SLAP!* that made me jump. The air inside the room was thick and sticky and almost unbearably warm. The swamp cooler was out and two small electric fans barely moved, much less cooled, the summer afternoon air.

Aunt Lucille, a bright pink smock over her caftan, stood over the wet head of an immense, very black woman of indeterminate age (somewhere between fifty and a hundred), her mountainous body covered from the neck down with a plastic sheet. Aunt Lucille's rubber-gloved hands had been massaging something into the big woman's hair. She froze in midmassage at the sight of me, looking at me with what might well have been expectation. The big woman looked at me too, as did Athena — perched on a low stool, pushing at a tiny, light-skinned woman's cuticles with a little wooden stick. The little lady with the cuticles looked too. I stood in the doorway for a moment, feeling the pounding of my heart behind my eardrums, catching my breath.

Suddenly, Aunt Lucille applied a smile to her face much as a woman might apply lipstick (only considerably faster, I imagine), and said, "Junie. You're back so soon. Did you have a nice visit with your daddy? How's my poor baby brother feeling today? Lord, such a shame! Seems the good they do die young. How you feeling, cher? You hungry, baby?"

I watched my aunt's smile quiver at the corners as I walked slowly and deliberately toward her. I stopped as close to Aunt Lucille as I could without actual physical contact, drew myself up to full height (such as it is), and allowed the gospel music from the boom box on the counter to hang in the air a moment before saying, quietly but clearly, "He didn't send for me."

"What?" came Athena's voice from about knee level.

"He doesn't want to see me," I said, speaking around the rapidly expanding lump in my throat. "I can't believe you'd do this," I said and took half a step back toward the door.

"Muh?" Athena stood up to face her mother.

"Junie—" Aunt Lucille lifted a gloved, chemical-coated hand from her customer's head.

"Junie?" said the big woman in the chair. "Junie? This can't be little Junie," she said, a big grin splitting her round, sweat-shiny face. "Not L.J.'s li'l bitta boy."

"Sure is," Aunt Lucille announced with a smile, obviously relieved at the interruption. "Junie, you remember Miss Lynn-Yvette Mayall."

The corpulent Miss Lynn-Yvette grinned anew beneath her head of wet hair and said, "You remember me, cher?"

I managed a small smile and a little lie. "Of course I do, ma'am. How've you been?"

"Child," said Lynn-Yvette, drawing the word out in a lengthy fermata, "last I saw you, you wasn't nothing but a little bitta boy. You here to see after your daddy?"

"Yes, ma'am."

"Sho' is a shame about your daddy," she said, the smile briefly leaving her face. It returned quickly as Lynn-Yvette looked me up and down, then fluttered coquettish lashes and added, "You sho' grew up into a good-lookin' young man, yeah."

Miss Lynn-Yvette's flattery managed to bring a genuine smile to my lips. "Thank you, ma'am," I said.

"Spittin' image of his daddy," she said, as if I'd suddenly left the room.

I felt an involuntary cringe. It was a decidedly bittersweet fact of my life that, while I had not seen my father in the flesh in over a decade, I saw traces of him, vague, incomplete images of him, every time I passed a mirror. While my coffee-with-Coffee-Mate skin color and prominent Native American cheekbones come courtesy of my mother, I walk this earth on scaled-down reasonable facsimiles of Lance Rousseau's wide, flat, 10-double-E feet (mine are size 9s). My smile is his smile, down to the slight overlap of one incisor over its neighbor on the left side of my mouth. And my overall body build is a replica of Lance's: long legged, high waisted, big armed, frustratingly difficult to fit in men's ready-to-wear. Again, somewhat scaled down, but again, unmistakably Lance. My brother David got our father's relatively fair complexion and light eyes. I got his high-set ass and his uneven hairline and pro-nounced widow's peak.

My anger somewhat defused, I suddenly felt weary to the bone. I breathed a sigh that felt like water in my lungs. "I'll talk to you later, dearest aunt," I said to Aunt Lucille, then smiled and said, "Pleasure to see you again, Miss Mayall."

"Good to see you, cher," called Lynn-Yvette as I turned and walked away. I heard Athena speak my name, but chose to ignore her. I had one foot out the door when I barely heard Miss Lynn-Yvette Mayall say, "Lord, that's some kind of pretty boy. Spittin' image of his daddy."

"Shut up, Lynn-Yvette," snapped Aunt Lucille, and the screen door slammed ka-SLAP! and the Swan Sil-vertones crooned sweet words of comfort to Mary and her sister Martha. Oh, Mary, don't you weep. Oh, Mary, don't ask!

"What's up, Captain?" Nigel was waiting just outside the beauty shop door when I emerged, his eyes wide with what looked like a combination of curiosity and concern.

I continued toward the house, Nigel keeping up beside me. "My beloved aunt, your grandmother," I said, taking on the clipped "Masterpiece Theater" inflection that often comes with anger, "has brought me here under false pretenses." I stomped up the back stairs and let myself into the kitchen.

"Shot who?" Nigel shut the back door behind him and leaned against it, looking askance.

"Aunt Lucille called me three days ago. 'Yo' daddy's dyin',' she said. 'He's asking for you, cher. He needs to see his li'l baby boy before he goes home to Glory.'" I turned, and opened the big old Frigidaire and stood in the cool of its insides for a moment while I looked for something cold to drink. "And like a fucking fool," I said into the fridge as I reached for a gallon bottle of Sparkletts water, "I drop everything, take vacation time from work, jump on a plane — which, by the way, I hate worse than just about anything — and run to the old man's bedside for the big reconciliation scene." I shoved the refrigerator door shut and turned back to Nigel. "And do you know what that wasted old sonofabitch said to me?" I uncapped the bottle of water and, feeling spiteful and a little bit naughty, drank directly from the bottle. I swallowed a series of audible gulps, the water blessedly cool down my throat and chest and belly. "'What are you doing here,' he says. Looking like I'd just emptied a bedpan in his face. 'What are you doing here?'"

The closing of the throat, the burning of the eyes were upon me before I knew it. "You know who he asked for? David," I said. "Dear, dead David." I raised the water bottle toward my mouth, then lowered it. "Shit,"

I said as the first tears fell. "Would you just look at me," I said, as much to myself as to Nigel. "I'm a grown man, for god's sake. I'm almost thirty-five god-damn years old, and I'm crying all the god-damn *time!*"

"Hey, Cap." Nigel approached me slowly. I wanted my handkerchief in the worst way, but I couldn't seem to decide how to get to it with the water bottle in one hand and the bottle cap in the other. "Here," Nigel said, relieving me of both bottle and cap. I had just managed to fish my ever-damp handkerchief out of my pocket when Aunt Lucille entered the room through the back door, gloveless but still in her smock, emotion stretching her facial features along the horizontal. Athena, looking confused, cuticle stick still in her hand, followed her mother in.

"Junie—," Aunt Lucille began.

Athena interrupted: "What is going on here?"

"I'm sorry, cher," Aunt Lucille said, moving toward me with her hands outstretched as if to prove she was carrying no weapons. "You know I meant well."

"You *meant* well?" I heard my voice squeak through my sore throat. "You had no right," I said, jabbing a forefinger in my aunt's direction. "You had no right to do that."

"Do what?" attempted Athena.

"He's your daddy," Aunt Lucille said, reaching out a hand, stopping just short of touching my face, then pulling back. "I thought you should be here."

"Would somebody in this kitchen please tell me what's going on?" shouted Athena, finally commanding her relatives' attention. Nigel, still cradling the Sparkletts bottle in his hands, spoke up first.

"I think I can field this one," he said. He looked first to me, then to his grandmother; neither of us responded. For me, I'd been over it once — I was only too happy to let Nigel take the floor. "Correct me if I'm wrong here," he began, "but it looks to me like Queenie got the Captain to come down here by telling him his daddy asked to see him just one more time before he died. And as it turns out" — Nigel treated his grandmother to an accusatory glance — "he never did. And when Uncle L.J. saw the Captain here, he threw him out the room. As much as you can throw somebody out of a room when you're strapped to a bed." He turned to me and raised one thick dark eyebrow. "That about cover it?"

I nodded and very nearly smiled. "Yep."

Hands on hips, Athena shook her head and said, "Oh, Muh."

Aunt Lucille smiled lamely and said, "Why don't we all sit down."

I crossed my arms over my chest, wet hanky clutched in one fist, and said, "If it's all the same to everybody, I'd rather stand."

"All right, dad-gummit," Aunt Lucille shouted, planting fists to hips, "stand, then!" She dropped her hands to her sides, took a chest-filling breath, then let it out. She said, so softly as to be nearly inaudible, "Lord, ha' mercy today." Then, to me, a sad little half smile on her lips, she said, "Yes, Junie, I lied. Your daddy didn't ask to see you. He's way too big a hard-headed jackass to do that. But I just knew when he saw you there at that bedside..." She looked down at the floor, shook her head. "I thought a father and his son..." She shrugged. "I was wrong. I'm sorry." She looked back up into my face and added, "Can't say the old gal didn't mean well."

My initial impulse was to take my aunt into a big hug, give her credit for good intentions, tell her it was all right. But at the moment, I was more in the mood to spread the hurt around a little, so I employed a hushed, dramatic tone and said, "It's probably too late to try to get a flight out of Lake Charles tonight. I'll leave in the morning." I left the kitchen without another word, confident I'd created the desired effect. Rounding the corner into the sewing room, I heard Aunt Lucille call my name and Athena say, "Muh, would you just let him be."

I was safe between the headphones, flat on my back on the too-soft double bed in the too-warm back bedroom, my arm across my eyes and a smile beginning to soften the corners of my mouth as Billie sang "Swing, Brother, Swing" directly into my head. It was the gentle but insistent swing of the Count Basie Band (1937-vintage), live from the Savoy Ballroom (stompin' at the Savoy, indeed) and the raspy, world-worn alto of Lady herself, managing to cool my overheated brain in a way the swamp cooler sweating and roaring above me could not begin to cool my moist, prickly skin. Lady didn't always sing the blues. When the mood struck her, she could swing like sixty. And nothing short of a shot of Cuervo or a gram or two of tryptophane — not yoga breathing, not visualization, not deep, focused meditation in which I surround myself in white light and reaffirm my position as a beloved child of the Universe — pushes the saw-toothed man-eating hellhounds of emotion away from my throat like Lady Day swingin' on the Walkman.

I asked Dennis once why a man born all but simultaneously with rock and roll should, in the midst of his life's most emotionally harrowing episode to date, find refuge, solace, succor in the sound of music performed and recorded some twenty and more years before. Why not the music of my own childhood and increasingly remote youth, but the music of my parents' childhoods? Why Basie and Billie and the Ellas — Ella Fitzgerald, Ella Johnson of the Buddy (her big brother) Johnson Band and Ella Mae "the Cow-Cow Boogie Girl" Morse? Why not the Beatles, the Supremes, Freddie and the goddamn Dreamers?

Dennis shrugged, did his patent-pending inscrutable look, and said, "What difference does it make, as long as it makes you feel better?"

For this I'm paying $150 a fifty-minute hour. Well, the thirty percent my medical insurance doesn't cover, anyway.

At the touch on my arm, I cried out ("Hah!") and jackknifed up in bed, victim of the unavoidable startle so common to the headphone addict. Nigel stood at the side of the bed, his brow crimped, his lips attempting a smile. "Sorry," Nigel said, not entirely audible over Billie and one solidly swingin' horn section. I pulled the phones from my ears in time to hear Nigel say, "You wanna go for a ride?"

Giving the matter absolutely no thought, I shrugged and said, "Sure."

"Me and Junie goin' for a ride," Nigel called out to no one in particular, and did not await a reply as he preceded me through the front door.

I sighed one of my all-too-frequent audible sighs as Nigel started the car and the air-conditioning kicked in, the first blasts of air musty-smelling but oh, so cool. I sighed for the feel of my moist shirt going cool against my skin, puckering my nipples, sighed for this sweet respite from 85 degrees and 80-some-odd percent humidity in a car with childhood memories tucked into the creases of the upholstery like lost nickels and dimes and Al Jarreau on the tape deck pulling and twisting notes like handfuls of Play-Doh. I closed my eyes, raised my arms, and grabbed the headrest behind my ears, enjoying the cool air in my armpits. "Where are we going?" I asked finally.

"Does it matter?" countered Nigel.

"Nah," I said, leaning back into the cool. After an elongated moment, just to make something resembling conversation, I said, "You know, you really shouldn't drink raw eggs."

"Shot who?"

"Athena tells me you've been sucking up raw eggs. Which is the best way we know of to get yourself a nice dose of salmonella poisoning. Which could kill you." I waited a moment for a reply, then opened my eyes and looked toward Nigel.

"Don't go," Nigel said, looking directly ahead.

"What?"

"Don't go," he repeated. "Stay."

A little smile pushed at the corners of my mouth. I didn't know what Nigel was getting to, but something about the deadly earnest look on my cousin's face made me smile. "Why not?" I asked.

Nigel braked for a stoplight. I wasn't sure if I'd already seen the strip mall out the passenger window, or if it looked exactly like one I'd already seen. "Well," Nigel said, "you're here already."

"No arguing that one," I agreed.

Nigel didn't crack a smile. "And I do realize your daddy has totally dissed you and you're stung. But just because he acted like an asshole don't mean he might not chill out some if you try again, right? I mean, you might as well finish what you came for, right? Besides," he added as the light went green and he hit the gas, "you go back to L.A. tomorrow, you go home to what?"

So much for my smile. The kid had a point. "Anything else?" I asked.

"I don't want you to go," Nigel said, his voice rising at the end of the sentence so it almost sounded like a question.

"Oh?" I said, my voice a bit squeaky, my heart doing a funky little drumroll.

"We're here," Nigel said, pulling the car over in front of a small wood-frame house (probably the same vintage as Aunt Lucille's house, though not even half the size) in dire need of paint. I followed Nigel to the front door, which Nigel opened as if he lived there, and inside.

Momentarily blinded by the abrupt change of light upon entering the dimly lit house, I paused just inside the doorway to allow my eyes to adjust inside somebody's rather cluttered, eclectically furnished living room. A 19-inch portable television sat atop an old wooden wire spool in one corner, its screen dark, facing a big, rambling sectional sofa whose color and pattern when new would have been difficult to discern. A Magnavox console stereo, all but identical to the one my parents had owned when David and I were little, stood against one wall, filling the room with the sound of the Stax house band and Rufus Thomas's cement mixer of a voice singing, "I'll show you how to Walk the Dog."

I didn't notice the two old men seated at the collapsible card table just to one side of the front door until one of them startled me by nearly shouting, in that peculiar overcompensating volume of the hard-of-hearing, "How you doin', Nigel?" When I looked, a very old, very black man in a faded, rather threadbare long-sleeved shirt and nondescript pants, smiled a toothless smile in our direction.

"Just fine, Mr. Freen," Nigel said, raising his voice several decibels higher than normal. "Evening, Mr.

Fitty," Nigel added for the benefit of the other old man. He was light skinned enough to pass for white, though presumably not, painfully thin, and bent like a question mark over the checkerboard on the table, his gnarled, veiny hands flat against the tabletop. "Evening, Nigel," he said, not looking up from the board.

"How's the game?" Nigel said, leaning toward the table.

"This old niggah cheatin'," Mr. Fitty said, still not moving his eyes from the board. "Gots to watch him every minute, yeah."

"Now you know I ain't never cheated, you ugly ol' Cajun," countered the still-smiling Mr. Freen.

"Y'all, this my cousin Junie," Nigel said, touching my shoulder lightly with his fingers. "My uncle L.J.'s son."

"Naw, it ain't." Mr. Fitty finally looked up from the checkerboard. "Not dis here growed-up man here." He held out a knotty hand and offered a smile which included very few teeth. "You better come on over here, shake your old uncle Fitty's hand."

I did as I was told. The old man's grip was surprisingly strong, his skin dry and crisp as parchment. "Boy, I been known you since you wasn't nothin' but your mama wantin' some vanilla ice cream and some sardines." He laughed a wheezy *heh-heh-heh.* "Don't remember me?" he said, still holding my hand. I shook my head no. "Been a long time," the old man said, releasing my hand. "Long time. Freen," he yelled as if his friend were across the street instead of across a card table, "Freen, this here L.J.'s boy."

"I heard," Mr. Freen said with an exaggerated expression of exasperation. "I can hear, y'old high-yella muthafucka." He grinned that dark crevice of a grin again and held out a dark, straight-fingered hand. I accepted it, and Mr. Freen clasped his other hand around mine and held it tightly. His hands felt cool and padded, like a brand-new chair. "Pleasure to meet you, young man," he said. "Yo' family sho' do make some nice-looking mens," he added, winking an eye.

"Thank you, sir," I said, stifling a laugh.

"You watch out for that black sumbitch," Fitty said, his eyes back on the checkerboard. "He like 'em young."

"Damn right," Freen said, looking up and speaking directly to me. Tugging on my hand, he brought my face over and down, closer to his own. "Lemme tell you somethin', baby," he said, his oddly sweet-smelling cologne filling my nostrils. "You ain't had none yet 'til you had it from a man wid no teeff." And he laughed a long high note, *HEEEEEEEE,* followed by a cluster of *hee-hee-hee*'s, before finally relinquishing my hand. I looked toward Nigel, who refused to meet my eyes.

"Where Anna Lee at?" Nigel asked the table at large.

Fitty replied, "She out in the back, getting some meat out the deep freeze."

"No, she ain't," said a high-pitched wind chime of a voice. I turned to see the owner of the voice walking toward me on tiny white-sneakered feet, every inch of five-foot-two, wearing light blue overalls and a man's white t-shirt, a smile dimpling a round face the color of baking chocolate, a full key ring attached to her overalls jingling like sleigh bells as she walked. "Nigel," she said in that incredible baby-doll voice, "this your new ya-ya?" I couldn't help smiling.

"Anna Lee," Nigel said, "this is my cousin, Junie. Johnnie Ray Rousseau."

"The singer?" Anna Lee cocked her head, a Medusa-like headful of dreadlocks corralled in a brightly colored scarf. "My pleasure," she said, holding her right hand up and out toward me. Her handshake was like that of a small but energetic man. "I have your album in my collection," she said.

"You sent Muh two copies," Nigel said, "and I absconded with one and gave it to Anna Lee."

"And I play it often," she added.

"Really?" I said, a smile spreading across my face.

"Sugar, Anna Lee don't never bullshit about good music," she said, reaching up to pat me on the cheek, as if I were a very large child. From the stereo, Rufus Thomas had given way to Mahalia Jackson ripping through "When the Saints Go Marching In." "Child, you can really blow. You still singing?"

Just the tiniest little schmertz. "Not recently," I said.

"Shame," said Anna Lee, then shrugged her small shoulders. "Well, welcome to my little home," Anna Lee said. I searched her smooth brown face for some clue as to her age, but she could have been thirty, or forty, or sixty. "Y'all hungry?" she asked.

"Not really, thank you," I said, although it was high time I'd had something to eat.

"Got some good-ass gumbo in the kitchen," she said in a singsong like Glinda the Good Witch getting funky.

"Could we have the guest room for a while, Anna Lee?" Nigel asked.

"Child!" She shot Nigel a look. "With your cousin?"

Nigel smiled sheepishly. "We just need to talk in private."

"If you say so," she said with another little shrug. "Go 'head, ain't nobody back there. Just put the sign out. After you finish you come back out here and have some of this good gumbo, hear me?"

■

"And just who, may I ask, is this Anna Lee person?" I asked, following Nigel down a narrow hall covered on both sides with ancient framed photographs, portraits of black, brown, and café-au-lait people staring blank-eyed through a disconcerted Johnnie Ray Rousseau and into eternity.

"Anna Lee's a friend of mine," Nigel said as he pushed open one of three doors on the right side of the hall. "She used to be my favorite high school English teacher. Now she's my friend. I do odd jobs around the house for her sometimes. And she lets me use her guest room sometimes. Come on," he said, and I followed him into a small bedroom. Nigel moved a "Do Not Disturb" card (obviously removed from some hotel somewhere) from the inside doorknob to the outside and shut the door behind us.

My immediate assessment of the room was that it seemed outwardly clean, if sparsely furnished — there was a chenille-covered double bed, a plain blond-wood bureau with a mirror and one wooden chair — rather like a room in a Motel 6. I stood just inside the doorway, trembling slightly with confusion and a vague sexual excitement. Nigel untied and kicked off his high-top Converse basketball shoes (not those big, puffy, hundred-plus-dollar things the kids were wearing in L.A., but the old-fashioned kind I remember having worn as a child, and which my most recent piano accompanist liked to wear in mismatched colors — red on the right foot, white on the left). Nigel plopped down and sat cross-legged near the head of the bed.

"This is a much better sit than the chair," Nigel said.

I didn't budge from where I stood. I could feel my heart beating up in my throat. "Cousin Nigel," I said slowly and carefully, "what exactly is going on here?"

Nigel grinned his bad-boy grin and said, "I didn't lie to Anna Lee. I brought you here 'cause I want to talk to you in private." He shrugged. "Okay?"

None too sure how okay this whole situation was, I nonetheless said, "Okay," and joined Nigel on the bed. Pulling off my shoes, looking down at my Nike's instead of at my cousin, I said (not quite a question), "So, you're gay."

"Truth to tell," Nigel said, "I've always preferred ... 'enchanted.'" He grinned that grin of his.

"Shit," I said, drawing the word out over three long syllables.

"Shit?" said Nigel through a little laugh. "What mean, shit?"

I opened my mouth to speak, but no sound came. What could I say? I was sitting Indian-style on a bed in some stranger's guest room on the outskirts of No-where, Louisiana, with my beautiful eighteen-year-old cousin, and the feeling was decidedly strange. Not the least of my problems was the fact that Nigel, having announced his gayness, was suddenly rendered even more attractive in my eyes than before. Never one of those gay men who lust after heterosexuals, I found the possibility of mutual sexual attraction considerably more seductive than the possibility of rejection, disgust, and bodily injury.

Whether it was the recent knowledge of my cousin's sexuality or something about the light in the room in which we sat (supplied by one inelegant fifties-vintage overhead light fixture and the last dregs of sunlight filtered through the dime-store window curtains), I found myself suddenly more cognizant than before of the voluptuous lump of my cousin's Adam's apple, the particular fullness of his florid lower lip, the cords of muscle in his forearms. The skin of Nigel's upper chest, exposed by the tank top he wore, dark brown and glossy as the belly of a chocolate Easter bunny, gave the impression that, should I have chosen to bite into my cousin, the boy might prove to be creme-filled. If Aunt Lucille smelled edible, Nigel looked it.

"Does your mother know?" I asked finally, my mouth having gone a bit dry.

Nigel said, "Yeah. We don't talk about it, but she knows." He laughed a little snort of a laugh. "I think she blames herself, for raising me in a house with just women in it. I don't believe in blame, me."

I shook my head slowly and said, "Blessed Mother of Us All." In my head, questions pushed ahead of other questions like teenagers in a movie line. Was there gay life out here in Bumfuck, Louisiana? Did Nigel have a steady boyfriend? Why the hell wasn't the boy hopping the first plane, bus, or boxcar out of this hick town?

Nigel beat me to the punch. "That why things so fucked-up between you and your daddy? Because you're gay?"

Pain like a cast-iron elbow pressing hard into my belly. "Yeah," I admitted through a tight jaw. One thing and another, I had managed to forget, however briefly, my reason for coming to Louisiana in the first place. To fly to the deathbed of the father who didn't want me, who'd told me to get out, go home. My throat constricted and my eyes burned from the residue of a lifetime's paternally inflicted hurt, and from the impotent frustration with the way the old man could still inflict that hurt, still bring tears. "You know—," I began, then thought better of it and said, "Never mind." Why go into all that shit? I considered my handkerchief, then wiped at the moistened corners of my eyes with the heel of my hand instead.

"What?" Nigel said, leaning in a little.

I sighed a long one. Did I really want to cover this kind of overly traveled territory here, now, and with Nigel, he of the severe haircut and the impossibly long, curling eyelashes? Well, maybe some of it.

"The fact is, he never liked me," I said. "My father. Maybe he loved me, for like five minutes, when I was a baby. But he never liked me. I was never his idea of a firstborn son." I made a little face. "Of course, I was never any man's idea of a firstborn son. Except maybe Harvey Fierstein."

"Were you girlish?" Nigel asked, leaning back against the headboard, cupping his hands behind his head.

"Oh, child," I said, averting my eyes from Nigel's biceps and armpits, "I was wildly effeminate. Rather play with a Barbie doll than a Tonka truck. Couldn't throw a ball to save my neck. Still can't. Couldn't fight. Still can't. Cried a lot. I haven't changed much." A little laugh.

I pushed myself farther up onto the bed and leaned against the floral-papered wall. Across the room, atop the dresser sat my double on the looking-glass bed. I spoke to my mirror self rather than toward Nigel. "You know what he used to call me sometimes? Trixie. Like if he caught me playing with my cousin Camille's dolls, he'd say, 'Get away from there, Trixie.'" I waited out the little schmertz.

"Then David came along, and suddenly Dad had a real boy for a son. David, as they used to say, was 'all boy.' Do people still say that? 'All boy'?" I continued without waiting for an answer. "David ran and jumped and got dirty and played Little League ball and all that shit. So, after David came along, Dad ignored me for the most part. There are worse things, I guess." I closed my eyes, bounced the back of my head against the wall, just hard enough to feel it.

"But it wasn't 'til David was killed that Dad really started to hate me. From the moment we learned David was dead, I could see it in Dad's eyes that—" I felt the tears coming, but I breathed them back, blinked them back. "That if one of his sons had to be blown away in a drive-by shooting in front a fast-food restaurant, then it damn well should have been me." I opened my eyes and finally turned to Nigel, who sat against the headboard, arms across his chest. "I don't think he's ever going to forgive me for being the one who lived."

"You don't really believe that," Nigel said softly.

I barked a mirthless laugh, *Ha!* "You obviously don't know my father," I said.

"So what are you doing here?" Nigel asked. "Why come all this way to see him?"

"He's my father," I said, not the least sure, even as I said it, why a chance genetic fact, a mere toss of Nature's dice, should braid a seemingly unbreakable cord stretching over hundreds of miles and over a dozen or more years; nowhere near sure exactly what I was doing here. "He's dying," I added. I felt my lips tremble and I blinked rapidly, trying to keep the tears back.

Nigel extended his arms toward me and said, "C'mere." I leaned away from Nigel's hands, an involuntary move, almost a reflex. "I was just going to hug you," Nigel said, lowering his arms. "Isn't that what y'all do in L.A.? Sit in hot tubs, drink Chardonnay wine, and hug each other all the time?"

"I'm sorry," I said. "It's just—" How to say this?

"Just what?" Nigel crossed his arms tightly across his chest.

I studied the backs of my hands for a moment. "I'm not sure it's such a good idea for me to have that kind of physical contact ... with you." I didn't look at Nigel until I'd finished the sentence.

"Zat a fact?" Nigel said, cocking his close-cropped head to one side.

"Look," I said, "I'm attracted to you, okay? I mean, physically attracted to you."

The smile returned to Nigel's face. "Then we've come to the right place, Captain," he said, slapping the bed beside him.

"No!" I said, surprising myself with my own vehemence.

"Yo, Cap," Nigel said, holding up a protecting palm. "Maybe I'm not understanding something here. So bear with me, if you will. You just said you're attracted to me. And I'm telling you right now, I'm stone attracted to you. So what seems to be the problem?"

"The problem?" The boy must be joking. I held up an index finger. "You're my cousin." Another finger. "You're just a kid, for cryin' out loud. And—" Three fingers. "Your mother would grind my balls for boudin if she even dreamed I'd laid a hand on you." I thumped my head against the wall again. "'What's the problem,' he says."

"You serious with that shit?" Nigel said.

"Of course I'm serious," I said.

Nigel shook his head, rolling his eyes heavenward. "Fine," he said. "Really. Not like I need to force myself on nobody. But lemme tell you something." He held up a finger. "My mama ain't got nothin' to do with this." Two fingers. "Cousin don't mean shit. Not like one of us was a woman or something and we was gonna make feeble-minded little black babies. And—" Nigel wagged three fingers in the air. "I ain't no kid. I'm old enough to drink, vote, and march my black ass off to war. And I'm grown enough to know what I want. Which just might be more than I can say for other people in this room." He punctuated this last with a head nod and a pointed look, then settled back against the headboard, arms crossed.

I looked at Nigel. I looked at my mirrored self. I felt more than a little silly. All the kid had ever offered was a hug. "Is that hug still available?" I said.

"I don't know," Nigel replied. "I'm not sure it would be such a good idea for us to maintain such close physical proximity. We might turn to salt or something."

"Oh, shut up and hold me," I said, scooting myself backward between Nigel's outstretched legs, against my cousin's hard, flat front and into his arms.

After a moment, Nigel said, "Can I ask you something?"

"Sure." Anything, I thought, just keep hugging.

"Why don't you sing anymore?"

I waited out the tiny pinprick pain in the center of my chest near my heart, then said, "It's just not there anymore. When Keith—" A bigger pain, a penknife. "It's just not there anymore," I repeated, hoping Nigel would let it drop.

Nigel rubbed my chest with his palm in a little slow circle. "I see," he said, and nuzzled the back of my head.

And his beard is tickling the nape of my neck.

"Keith!" I'm giggling like a kid on the upswing of a seesaw. "Baby, you're tickling me."

We're sitting on the beach in Venice, in the summertime, on the blanket we bought in Puerto Vallarta in the spring. I'm cross-legged and just a bit hunched forward; Keith is wrapped around my back like a big, warm cloak, his skin hot and sticky against my own, his muscular arms around my shoulders, his hands stroking up and down my forearms. Keith's legs, thick and covered with sun-bleached fuzz, form a fence around mine, his feet resting sole-to-sole in front of mine.

I'm holding one of Keith's big feet in each of my hands and massaging the deep arches with my thumbs as we lean into one another, laughing and cuddling, oblivious to the dozens of people around us.

And he's kissing my ear. And making me cry.

Crying.

"That's okay, baby," Nigel said, folding his long, sinewy arms around me and holding me close against him.

"I'm sorry," I blubbered, tears and snot falling freely from my face, since I couldn't reach my handkerchief from my present position.

We sat for maybe half an hour more, not talking, just sitting and hugging. After a while, after the crying stopped, after I'd wiped my face and caught my breath, after I'd steadied myself against my cousin, I could feel the hot lump of Nigel's hard-on hot against my tailbone, and my own dick straining against the confines of my Levi's.

He didn't mention it, and neither did I.

Finally, Nigel said, "We best be getting back to the house."

■

Aunt Lucille was at the stove, stirring a great pot of seafood-smelling something (okra gumbo with shrimp was my immediate guess) when I followed Nigel through the front door. She turned and said, "Junie."

I stopped. "Ma'am?"

Aunt Lucille tap-tap-tapped her spoon on the rim of the pot and set it on the stovetop. Wiping her hands on a dishtowel, she came to the kitchen door. "Junie," she said, an attempt of a smile on her lips, "you still angry with your old aunt Lucille?"

I shook my head. "No."

Aunt Lucille brought her towel-holding hand toward her heart in a characteristically stagy gesture. "You forgive me?"

"Nothing to forgive," I said.

Aunt Lucille's face split into a smile. "Bless your heart," she said, gathering me into her arms in a surprisingly forceful hug. "I do hate to see you go so soon," she said, letting me go.

"I've changed my mind," I said. "I'm going to stay around for a while. Might as well finish what I started."

Aunt Lucille smiled a fresh smile, swept me into another hug, and said, "Bless your heart. Bless your little heart."

6.

I had the Dream again that night.

The hall.

Moving slowly, inevitably toward the end of the hall, toward the gurney. Legs stiff and motionless, but still moving, as if on a conveyor belt, as if on a moving walkway at an airport. As if in a dream.

And I knew it was a dream. "This is a dream," I said from somewhere outside the figure moving down the hall, seemingly powerless to stop the movement toward the horror I knew waited against the wall at the far end. "I can stop this," the outer me told my moving self. "I read it in that book Dennis loaned me. I can control my dreams." But still I moved closer to the gurney, the gurney moved closer to me. I covered my face with hands that proved transparent — I could still see the gurney clearly, moving toward me. I watched the sheet covering the battered body begin to inch down, uncovering the top of the head.

And I screamed, "No!" Screamed both inside and outside the moving figure, eyes shut tight but unable to lose sight of the thing at the end of the hall. And again: "No!" And again. And again.

"No!" I shouted once more, before I realized the gurney was gone. My eyes were closed and there was darkness, the relief of nothingness. My eyes opened and still it was dark. I was sitting up in a bed. Whose? Where? My naked arms and chest and back were wet and suddenly cold. I trembled violently, my teeth clicked together like castanets played by a palsied Spaniard. My eyes darted about, slowly acclimating to the dark. The back bedroom. Aunt Lucille's house. My heartbeat was a boxer's leather-gloved fist slamming against my rib cage again and again, throbbing against my throat, behind my ears, my breath whistling through my esophagus, in and out of my open mouth, drying my lips.

"Johnnie?" A soft, familiar voice, close to my side.

"Keith?"

A whisper: "It's me — Nigel."

A warm hand on my shoulder. Body smells I had already come to find comfortable, comforting. I grabbed Nigel's wrist, held it tightly. "Hey," Nigel said, climbing knees-first onto the bed. I released Nigel's wrist, reaching for him with both arms, a desperate cornered-animal noise escaping my throat. "Hey," Nigel said, "hey," his voice soft and high as if talking to a newborn, his breath hot and sour from sleeping. "It's okay, baby. It's okay."

Nigel pressed gently against my shoulders, pushing me back against my dampened pillow, and stretched out full-length on top of me, covering me, his face against my right ear, whispering, "It's okay." I held Nigel around the middle of his back, the young man's warmth, his weight, his whispered words slowly soothing and calming me. I felt my heartbeat decelerating toward normal, felt the fisted muscles in my shoulders and behind my legs relax and soften, felt and heard my breath move more quietly through me, brushing past my vocal chords on my outbreath, making a soft hum.

"Thank you," I whispered up toward the ceiling.

"Anything for you, Captain," Nigel said, so softly I never would have heard the words if Nigel's lips hadn't been so close to my ear as to be nearly touching it. When the warm, moist tip of Nigel's tongue made contact with the shell of my ear, I started, tensed, gasping in an audible breath. "Relax," Nigel whispered.

Nigel rolled to one side of me, one leg across my hips — the narrow single bed barely containing the both of us — and stroked soft, warm circles up and down my chest and belly with his broad-palmed hand. I felt my skin vibrate like the filament in a light bulb under Nigel's touch, felt my nipples awaken and my spine involuntarily arch, even as a nagging gnome voice at the base of my skull, a voice simultaneously similar to my mother's, my father's, and Athena's, said, You shouldn't be doing this. You shouldn't be letting your cousin lay all over you like this. Rubbin' on you and kissin' on you. You shouldn't. Then Nigel danced his fingertips over my nipples, making them jump up and shout, Hey! like two little James Browns. And suddenly I thought, "Fuck 'shouldn't.'"

"What?" Nigel said.

"Nothin'," said I and took in a breath through my teeth as Nigel sucked on my earlobe and then gently nibbled at it. I rubbed the long-muscled boyleg bisecting my body, massaging it from knee to haunch, and humped my hard-on against the humid skin of Nigel's inner thigh, while Nigel ground his hot, sticky boner against my hip. I tugged at Nigel's leg and whispered, "Lie on top of me again."

Nigel said, "Yeah."

I tasted the wet, raw-meat taste of my cousin's long, muscular tongue, sucked it, slurped it, chewed on it; I kissed my cousin's thick lips, licked his stubbly jaw and his quivering eyelids, xylophoned my tongue back and forth across his teeth. Nigel took my lower lip into his mouth and worried it between his teeth, then set it free and tried the other one, then back again, finally settling into a quick, pistoning tongue-fuck in and out of my mouth in ragged counterpoint to the up-and-down of his hips. I kneaded great handfuls of Nigel's hard-muscled teenage ass, pushing and tugging at the slippery mounds of muscle, fingering along the deep cleft, poking an exploratory middle finger against the lumpy button of Nigel's anus, feeling the big buttocks tense and relax beneath my fingers with the steady pantomime of fucking that shoved the underside of Nigel's boner over and over along the groove between my thigh and balls. I met the movement of Nigel's hips with my own, pushing my pelvis against my cousin's groin, massaging my balls and dick against my cousin's crotch in a belly-to-hard-flat-belly horizontal hoochie-coochie of big brown-skinned boners slip 'n' slidin' up and down and around between bodies warm and wet and simultaneously slippery and sticky with sweat and the stuff steadily leaking from the blood-bloated noggin of Nigel's hard-on.

I suddenly gasped, my entire body stiffened, as if someone had jumped out from the dark and yelled, "Boo!" and my balls pulled up against my pelvis so hard they ached and my dick splattered my own throat and chest and belly with come and my head filled with white noise but I could just hear Nigel's voice in one ear saying, "Yeah, baby," saying something about hot stuff, saying something about big-ol' dick. I trembled with violent aftershocks while Nigel maneuvered one hand between his body and mine, nuzzling and nibbling my neck as he pulled his penis to orgasm, growling and snorting like some sort of beast and more than doubling the volume of milky liquid splashed across my front.

Nigel whispered something like "Oh, baby" and lowered his full weight back onto me, making a loose, wet, flatulent sound as wet chest and belly made contact with wet chest and belly. I felt the smile spread across my face as I stroked big stripes up and down Nigel's back.

■

I woke up to the morning sun shining warm and red through my eyelids, legs entangled in the damp sheets, feeling like a song by the Ronettes, a vibrating, fairly humming hard-on between my legs. I reached out an arm and, finding myself alone in bed, I briefly wondered if I'd dreamed it all. Touching my belly, I found no telltale crust on my skin. I brought my hands up to my face and breathed in. My fingers and palms smelled of sweat and semen and Nigel's Mennen Speed Stick deodorant.

I had obviously fallen dead asleep in Nigel's arms without so much as a thank-you and nighty-night. I could imagine Nigel grinning that nasty-boy grin of his and chortling to himself as he wiped our collective bodily juices from both our chests and stomachs. I hadn't awakened again during the night. And I could remember no more dreams.

I turned over onto my belly and stretched like a cat, rubbing my hard dick into the mattress, smiling to myself and moaning softly, reveling in the exquisite pain-pleasure of the stretch and my boner, and the recent memory of my cousin's taut young body, his kiss, his cock. It had been so long since I'd felt like this. So damn long. Rolling over onto my back, the warm, dark scent of coffee found my nostrils and I knew I must answer its call. After another long, back-arching, vertebra-popping stretch, I recited the Twenty-third Psalm (up to "Surely goodness and mercy") to expedite the deflation of my boner, then slid out of bed like an omelette out of a Teflon pan.

■

"Well, look who decided to get on up." Athena smiled her too-even smile over the top of a steaming coffee mug as I approached the open kitchen doorway, freshly showered and dressed in jeans and an "I ♥ Tortola" t-shirt purchased on the last vacation Keith and I had taken together. At the sight of Athena, looking small and girlish in the morning light, barefoot and wearing what seemed to be one of Nigel's old school gym jerseys (a rather threadbare blue-and-yellow thing with "Lake Charles" emblazoned across the front), I suddenly felt guilt like a lead bagel in my belly. What would she think of me if she knew what had happened between Nigel and me the night before? What would she say?

She said, "You hungry? I could fix you some grits and eggs."

"No, thanks," I said. Actually, I was ravenous, but I couldn't abide the thought of Athena slaving over a hot stove on a hot morning after what I'd recently committed with her only child.

"Don't you have to feed them big-ol' muscles?" Athena said through a smile.

"I'll just have a couple of bananas or something," I said.

"How 'bout some coffee?" Athena said, indicating the big old GE electric percolator on the kitchen counter. "Just made."

"Please," I managed to rasp, still standing in the doorway, not yet able to enter the room. Athena put down her cup, rose from the table, and pulled another cup from an upper cabinet.

"Nigel," she said, and I flinched at the sound of my cousin's name from his mother's lips, "Nigel be back to take you to the hospital soon. He's down to Anna Lee's place." She overfilled the cup, spilling coffee on the counter and her fingers. "Shit," she said, setting down cup and coffeepot, quickly adding, "excuse my French." It has long puzzled and amused me that people — including people of French descent, no less — excuse themselves after swearing by saying, "Excuse my French." She ran cold water from the tap over her fingers.

"Little heifer teach school down to Lake Charles. Nigel call himself being her friend," Athena said. "He cleans her place up for her, does odd jobs and all that jazz. More'n he'll do for me." Blotting the counter with a dishtowel, she said, "If Muh knew what go on in that woman's house, she'd have a stroke." The lead bagel in my stomach split and divided like an amoeba. "Drinking," Athena continued, rinsing the dishtowel, "gambling. Good thing Muh don't hardly go out the house."

"Where is Aunt Lucille?" I asked.

"Sitting in the bed, drinking coffee, watching Sally Jessy Raphael. She got them transvestites on the show again. Seem like every time you turn around, she got transvestites on. You take cream and sugar in your coffee, don't you?" Athena asked, turning to bring the cup to the table. Looking to find me still standing in the doorway, she applied hand to hip and said, "You comin' in, or what?"

"Black, please," I said in what I hoped would pass for a normal conversational tone, taking a step into the kitchen, hoping my guilt wasn't scrawled across my face like a homemade tattoo. Taking the chair across the table from Athena's, I lifted my cup with a rather unsteady hand and blew into it hard enough to splash coffee like little brown raindrops onto the newspaper spread across Athena's side of the table.

"I was pretty sure you and Nigel were gonna get along," Athena said. I stared into my coffee, watching tiny drops of oil floating along the dark brown surface. Attempting a sip, I scalded my upper lip and quickly set the cup down onto the table.

"He's a nice kid," I said, stretching my face into something I hoped would pass for a smile.

"He's crazy about you," Athena said, lifting her cup toward her lips. "He was up this morning scrambling eggs. Said Junie said not to eat 'em raw. Like I haven't been saying that all the time." She sipped her coffee, closing her eyes as if savoring the aroma and flavor of it. Opening them again, she said, "It sure is good to see you, Junie. It's been too long." She set her cup down onto the newspaper. "You know," she said, "I've always felt real close to you. I mean, even when we were kids, even though I was older and you were a boy. I always felt like we were friends."

That made me smile, really smile. "Me too," I said.

"Rilly?"

"Yes," I said. "Really." And indeed, I had long felt a strange sort of spiritual bond between Athena and myself, a closeness despite the miles that separated us and our too-infrequent meetings.

"You always seemed, even as a kid, you seemed — not just smart, though Lord knows you was always smart. You seemed..." She searched the kitchen ceiling for a word. "Wise," she said finally.

"Wise," I said through a little chuckle. "Now, I've been called a lot of things, but never that. Sure you don't mean wise-ass?"

"No, rilly," Athena said. "You remember when I got pregnant with Nigel? Not even through school yet. Not married, not gettin' married. You were the only person in the whole family who didn't give me an ounce of shit." She sipped coffee. "Everybody was on my ass — Muh,

Uncle L.J., even Clara, who I could usually count on to be on my side. But not you. I remember you walked in on me and Muh, arguing about the pregnancy. And Muh was talkin' about my child being illegitimate. And I remember you popped up and said, 'No child is illegitimate if it's loved.'" She tapped her fingernails against the side of her cup. "Just like that. You weren't but — what? — fifteen years old? 'No child is illegitimate if it's loved.' Stopped Muh dead in her tracks. You remember that?"

"No," I had to admit. I didn't remember any such incident, and it surprised me to think I could have come up with such a statement at an age when my own knowledge of love and sex was sketchy at best, a time when my own sexuality was just beginning to peek out like a monster from under the bed.

"Well, that's just how it happened," Athena said. "That's what I mean when I say 'wise.'" She got up and poured herself another cup of coffee, then added, "Nigel is that way, too."

"Nigel is *what* way, too?" Nigel said, entering the kitchen from the living room, looking so delectable in a pair of old sawed-off blue jeans, his high-top sneakers, and a very flattering jacket of sweat that I felt my dick stir like an awakened sleeper at the sight of him. Nigel's eyes met mine, for just a splinter of a second; the looks and the small, secretive smiles we exchanged simultaneously warmed, excited, and embarrassed me. I wondered if Athena could somehow tell how special her son and I had become to one another over the past several hours: see it in our faces, smell it on our skins.

"None of your business," Athena said, leaning against the counter. She took a little sip of coffee and said, "And you can put a shirt on, ain't nobody impressed."

I watched Nigel's smile fall and his posture stiffen. Nigel looked quickly toward me and then back to his mother. "I wasn't trying to impress nobody," he said. "It's hot and I been workin', if that's all right with you."

Athena put her cup down so hard I was surprised it didn't break, and wagged a motherly finger in Nigel's direction. Both her offhand remark to Nigel and her reaction to his insubordinate reply reminded me so much of my own mother that I had to hold back a smile, in spite of the rising tension between Athena and her son.

"Don't be takin' no attitude with me, little boy," she said. "You ain't so big I can't whip your high butt."

Nigel's big eyes nearly doubled in size and a deep breath expanded his rib cage, increasing his bulk. He glanced quickly at me and then quickly back to Athena. I could all but see the words forming on Nigel's lips and without giving nearly enough thought to the possible consequences of walking into the crossfire created by a mother and son, I stood up and said, "I'd like to go to the hospital now, please."

Nigel deflated, looked quizzically at me as I moved toward him. "What?" Nigel said.

"Could we go now, please?" I said, gently but firm-ly guiding my cousin toward the front door with a hand between his shoulder blades. "We're going now, Theenie," I called over one shoulder, my voice full of forced lightness and cheer. "We'll see you later."

"Junie—" Athena made a weak attempt to call us back.

"Gotta go," I said in a campy singsong, "busy-busy, kiss-kiss!"

"God, she pisses me off sometimes," Nigel said as I shoved the front door shut behind us.

"She's your mother," I said, massaging the back of Nigel's neck with one hand for a fast moment. "Pissing you off is the sole reason she exists." I immediately felt sweat burst like popcorn on my forehead and begin its tickling way down the center of my back. "God," I said, blotting my face with my handkerchief, "why does it have to be so fucking hot all the time?"

I leaned face-first into the air-conditioning as Nigel backed the Blue Bomb out of the garage. Nigel said, "Thanks for getting me out of there, Cap."

"I don't know about you and Theenie," I said into the air-conditioning vent, "but when Clara and I go at it, we can make the Gulf War look like a slight difference of opinion. Retreat seemed the better part of valor. Or however the saying goes."

"You sure you want to go right to the hospital?" Nigel asked.

"What do you mean?" I looked up from the air vent.

"Well," Nigel said through one of those smiles of his, "we could stop at Anna Lee's. I just unstopped her bathroom sink, so she owes me a favor." He wiggled his eyebrows like a chocolate Groucho. "Whaddaya say, Cap'm?"

The lead bagel of guilt threw an impromptu party for a few close friends in the pit of my stomach. "Nigel," I began carefully, "what happened, what we did last night..."

"Yeah?" Nigel's smile drooped, as if he knew what was coming.

I took a deep breath and used most of it to say, "We can't do that anymore."

"Aw shit, man." Nigel thumped the back of his head against the headrest. "Tell me we ain't gonna start that again."

"Look," I said, turning to Nigel, watching the sour look on my cousin's face, "last night was wonderful for me. I needed it. And I'm grateful you were there. But—"

"But!" Nigel shouted.

"But," I continued, trying to keep my vocal volume within the conversational, "I just don't feel right about having sex with you, certainly not in your mother's—" Nigel was silently mocking me, flapping his lips up and down rocking his head from side to side. I felt anger rise like a zipper up the center of my chest, felt like an adult trying to reason with a petulant child, felt more than a little foolish for allowing myself to roll around with Nigel in the first place, and for the undeniable schoolboy crush I had allowed myself to fall into like a blind man into a mud puddle. "Pull over," I said through a tight jaw.

"You're the boss," Nigel said, turning the car sharply to the right and skidding to a stop.

"I thought I was dealing with a nineteen-year-old man," I said. "Obviously, I'm dealing with a nineteen-year-old boy."

Nigel made a shit-smelling face and said, "Oh, thanks. Really."

"Dammit, Nigel—" I wanted to slap him, spank him, take him by the shoulders, and shake him until he sounded like a maracas solo. "Why the hell won't you listen to me?"

"Say something that makes some kind of sense and maybe I will."

"All right," I said, "how about this? You know I like you. A lot. I'm more attracted to you than I remember being attracted to anybody in a long time."

"I feel a 'but' coming on," Nigel said.

"Yeah." I suppressed a smile. "But. You're my cousin. You're my cousin Theenie's little boy. Jesus, kid! I held you on my lap when you were four, five years old."

"I know," Nigel said, more softly. "I remember. I still don't know what all that's got to do with anything."

I had to stop and think a moment. What exactly did Athena have to do with me and Nigel wanting to make love? "I wouldn't want to do anything to hurt your mother."

"Aw, man..." Nigel rolled his eyes so hard his entire head rolled.

"Would you hear me out, please?" I said. "Theen and I, we've been friends since we were kids. There's always been this ... connection between us. I remember how tough it was for her, getting pregnant, with no hint of a husband. I tried to be a friend to her. And later on, when I tried to tell her I was gay, she—" I laughed to myself, remembering.

"What?" Nigel said.

"She'd come down to L.A. to visit ... somebody. I don't remember, but I know she wasn't in town just to see me. I was only about twenty, maybe twenty-one years old. And she'd brought some truly monstrous dope — God, I don't believe I'm telling you this."

■

Athena and I were semi-reclining on opposite ends of the secondhand love seat I was passing off as a sofa. We were better than two-thirds through the chubby joint she had rolled in tiger-striped cigarette papers. Both of us slender and brown and sporting matching Afros, we must have looked rather like bookends.

The compact stereo on the floor against the opposite wall filled the room, and filled my head, with Stevie Wonder's *Songs in the Key of Life.*

"I don't want to bore you with it," I said to nobody in particular.

"What?" said Athena, twiddling the remainder of the joint absently between her fingers.

"Stevie," I said. "Who else but Stevie would say, 'I don't wanna bore you with it, but I love you'?"

"Junie," she said, grinning a mouthful of her original teeth, "you fucked up?"

I considered the question carefully before answering. "I guess so."

And suddenly, we were both laughing like lunatics — uncontrollable, convulsive, eye-watering, belly-aching laughs, until I could barely catch my breath. As the wave of pointless, stoned-out laughter receded, I wiped my teary eyes with the heels of my hands as Athena shoved the burning end of the cigarette into a nearby ashtray and said, "Perhaps we have had enough," eliciting a fresh bubbling-up of giggles from us both.

I'd never felt quite so close to Athena. And I knew, all at once I knew it was time to tell her.

I closed my eyes and breathed in a chestful of smoke-laden air and Stevie Wonder music (all synthesized strings, gospel voices singing "We Shall Overcome," Krishnas chanting *hare-hare* and tinkling finger cymbals) and with the outbreath said,

"Theenie?"

Athena, leaning back, eyes closed, seemingly breathing in Stevie as well, said, "Hm?"

"Theenie, there's something I want to tell you," I said, my heart drumming a combination of nervousness and marijuana-induced jitters.

Athena opened one eye and said, "Wha's that, babe?"

"Athena, I'm gay," I said. And, in case the locoweed had dulled my cousin's hearing or her perception, I repeated, "I'm gay."

Athena closed her eye again, nudged my leg with her sweat-socked foot, and said, "Child, I knew that."

"You did?" I said, sitting up straight. "Who told you?"

She opened her eyes, sat up to face me, smiled, and said, "Didn't nobody have to *tell* me, Junie. What'd you think — I ain't never met no gay dudes before? Most of my good buddies in college was gay dudes."

She shrugged and I could all but see the entire issue roll off her narrow shoulders. "I'm starving," she said. "Wanna go get some Fatburgers?"

■

"Just like that." I touched Nigel softly on the shoulder with my fingertips. "I love your mother very much," I said. "Her friendship, her respect, are very important to me. I don't want to jeopardize that relationship. Okay?"

Nigel's lips lifted into an equivocal little smile. He shook his head slowly, then said, "Let's get to the hospital."

7.

◆ "I'm here to see my father," I said to the same braided-haired nurse I'd seen the previous day. "Lance Rousseau." The nurse glanced at her wristwatch and then briefly down at the desk and said, "They givin' him his breakfast now. You can go on in if you want to."

Nigel said, "I'll wait over there," indicating the small waiting area.

Several long, deep yoga breaths failed to calm my racing heartbeat as I approached the door to my father's room. I should have hopped the first plane home when I had the chance, I thought. Well, maybe the first train.

"Please, Mr. Rousseau," came a plaintive female voice from within the room. "How can I feed you if you won't open your mouth?" From the doorway, I could see my father, propped up in bed with several pillows, his face set, jaw clenched, a food tray set before him. Bedside, perched on a high stool, spoon in hand, was a heavyset, caramel-colored young nurse's assistant.

"I said get away from me, girl," Lance growled through clenched teeth.

"Come on now, Mr. Rousseau," the woman repeated in a voice like honey-butter laced with arsenic, "just one bite."

"No!" Lance said, teeth together as if wired shut. "You eat it."

I smiled at the little drama, at my father's childish petulance, the woman's exasperation. Suddenly I was considerably less nervous. The brawny-armed disciplinarian who had left so many stripes on my thighs, the paragon of masculinity who had made me feel so inferior for so very long, the father who had turned me from his home — that man, or what was left of him — lay all but helpless in a hospital bed, refusing to eat his porridge. Fate had had to nearly flatten Lance Rousseau before I could feel I had anything resembling the upper hand, but this was definitely it.

"Let me give it a try," I said, stepping into the small, machine-dense room. The nurse's aide turned. Lance looked across the bed, across the room. Though Lance's eyes gave me nothing, I could have sworn I saw the threat of a smile pass, if briefly, across my father's tightly shut face. "I'm his son," I added for the woman's benefit. She looked at Lance, then back at me. Perhaps finding a family resemblance in my features, almost certainly happy to be relieved of duty, she shook the spoon clean, walked over, and handed it to me. "Good luck," she said, deadpan, and left the room.

Wiggling the spoon between my fingers, I strolled toward the bed. "Hello, Dad," I said, climbing onto the stool vacated by the nurse's aide. No visible or audible acknowledgment from the man in bed. So I said, "Hello, son, how nice of you to drop everything and schlep halfway across the United States to be treated like so much dog shit by your hateful homophobic asshole father. What a good, good son you are."

Lance blinked. I considered emptying the breakfast tray onto my father's head and fingerpainting obscenities across his hospital gown in strained squash, but thought better of it. I took a couple of yoga breaths and tried again.

"How are you feeling today, Dad?" I said. Lance continued to stare straight ahead. But after a moment, he said, "I'm dying. How the hell are you?"

I suppressed a smile. It wasn't much, but it was an answer. "Well," I said, "Garbo talks. How the hell am I, you ask. Well, let's see, now ... my lover was killed by a hit-and-run over a year ago and I'm still in mourning. I'm given to screaming nightmares, I've been taking an extremely habit-forming prescription drug just to keep my mind from flying apart like a New Year's party favor, and I don't know if I'll ever love again. I'm in therapy with a shrink who looks like Opie, and who tells me there's no formal timetable for grief. And right at the moment, I'm sitting in a hospital room in the middle of Nowhere City, Louisiana, staring at my dying father, who doesn't want to see me. I'm fine." It crossed my mind to mention that I'd recently made something very like whoopie with Lance's nearly nineteen-year-old nephew, but chose not to just yet.

Finding no discernible reaction from Lance, I waved the spoon I still held, made a pop-eyed, twisted-lipped Baby Jane Hudson face, and barked à la Bette Davis, "Time ta eat-cha BREAK-fast!" I scooped up a spoonful of orangish-brownish mush from one of the larger compartments of the food tray and held it toward my father's tightly closed lips. Lance continued to stare straight ahead, across the room and seemingly through the open doorway and into the hall. I raised the spoon high, then brought it slowly down in a long, wavy line. "Open up the hangar," I singsonged, "here comes the airplane." No reaction. "Come on, Dad," I said softly. "I know it doesn't look so good, but I'm sure it's good for you. You need to rally your strength, you know."

"What for?" Lance said, opening his lips just enough to allow the words to escape. "I'm gonna die anyhow."

"So die, already!" I shouted, slamming the spoon down onto the tray, causing the food to splatter, leaving a little sprinkling of orangish-brownish spots on my father's hospital gown. "Don't just lie there, staring out into space, talking through your teeth, throwing people out, and pointedly not eating anything. Die if you're going to die. I'm sure they could use the room, and besides — I personally can't wait to do the hokey-pokey on your grave and get on with what is laughingly called my life. So just die, okay?"

I was trembling by the time I'd finished that little tirade. I crossed my arms tightly over my ribs and waited for it to pass. When, to my surprise, Lance opened his mouth wide, eyes closed like a man about to have his gums poked by a particularly clumsy dental hygienist, I scraped up another spoonful of food and carefully introduced it into my father's gaping mouth. Lance closed his lips around the spoon, frowning at the taste of it. When I had withdrawn the empty spoon, Lance said, "You talk just like your mother. You always did."

I lifted another spoonful from the tray and said, "I'll take that as a compliment, thanks. Open." Lance took another spoonful of the indeterminate mush, then said through barely parted lips, "How is your mother?"

"She's fine," I said. I seriously considered adding something about my mother finally finding a man who treated her as she deserved, but let it go for the moment. Among the grab bag of ill feelings I was harboring for my father, I held a special grudge for the sexual infidelities — some surreptitious, others carelessly exposed, some spitefully flaunted — which had driven Clara Rousseau away from her husband after twenty-one years of marriage. Now, nearly fifteen years later, I enjoyed the idea that my father, no longer the handsome bronze charmer, without wife and decidedly without paramour, might finally have lived to regret his past actions.

"She still living with that Jew?" Lance said.

"Yes," I said with some satisfaction. "She and Daniel are in Paris at the moment. Paris, France," I added, hoping the thought of the wife he'd so stupidly allowed himself to lose, summering in the city of *toujours l'amour* with a red-haired gynecologist seventeen years her junior, might cause my father some small pain. Nothing excruciating; a nice little sting would do. I smiled and said, "She's very, very happy." I watched my father's jaw muscles tighten and knew the sting had stung. I've seldom been one for kicking a man when he's down, but I have to admit I was really enjoying this.

The better part of a minute passed before Lance said, so softly I could just hear it, "I loved that woman."

I failed to stifle a quick, high, Chihuahua-bark of a laugh. "Well, you always did have the oddest little ways of showing your affection." I scooped up another spoon-ful of food, held it toward my father's face, and said, "More?"

"No," Lance said through his teeth, his eyes shut tight, as if the food ceased to exist as soon as he couldn't see it.

A long minute went by. Then two. Lance lay there thinking thoughts I could only have guessed at: the loss of a good wife? the impending loss of life? the blandness of his hospital breakfast? For my own part, I spent the silence thinking about a question, one I'd waited years to ask. Just considering it brought on a case of the trembles so strong I had to lay down the spoon. I took a good, long breath and went ahead. "On the general subject of people you allegedly loved," I said, crossing my arms again tightly across my front in a self-hug, "do — did you love me?"

"What?" Lance said, his expression unchanged.

"Nothing," I said quickly, feeling a fool for asking, feeling frustrated for having to ask. "Never mind."

Lance's sudden attack of deafness, whether genuine or feigned, gave me the opportunity to backpedal, to approach the love question a bit more slowly and quietly, like a rabbit in your dahlia garden. "You always favored David so much," I began. "Not that I blame you. What father wouldn't have? He was everything a father could want in a son. Unlike some of us." My heart beat like a West Hollywood dance club on a Saturday night, but I forced myself to continue. "And I know I never brought home any basketball trophies, but I did excel in some things — my grades, my clarinet. My singing. But I —" I felt my throat tighten; I swallowed hard. "God, I must sound like Tommy Smothers, here. 'Dad always liked you best.' But, see, I never quite felt like you valued the things I did as much as you valued what David did. I so wanted to feel like you were proud of me, too. For the things I accomplished. And that you loved me, too." I paused a moment, waiting for some reaction from my father: if not some small morsel of belated reassurance, at least some knee-jerk denial of ever having withheld his approval or his love.

There I sat. Open. Vulnerable. Utterly unacknowledged.

Finally, I heard my father take in a breath through slightly parted lips.

"Proud of you," he said, neither opening his eyes nor turning his face in my direction, his voice a harsh rasp, like steel wool against your skin. The phrase emerged without inflection, not quite a question, not exactly a statement. It occurred to me that my father might be attempting to tell me that he was, in fact, proud of me, and I felt a slight adrenaline kick at the thought.

"You made me sick," he said, slowly, deliberately, his meaning quite unequivocal, each word hitting me like a roundhouse right to the stomach. "Come sashaying into my house," he continued, his lips scarcely moving, "talking about 'I'm gay,' like you so damn happy you was a faggot. Like I'm supposed to be happy about it. Bringing some little sissified white boyfriend right *in* my house. Like it wasn't enough, my son was taking some white man up the butt — I had to *meet* him, too." He made a little snorting sound around the plastic nose piece. "Proud of you," he repeated, then added, "shit."

I gripped the sides of the stool I sat on, fighting the shakes, blinking rapidly against the tears. I was *not* going to cry. I refused to give him the satisfaction of making me cry. A minute, maybe ninety seconds, and several long, deep breaths later, the trembling subsided and I decided to trust my voice not to betray my pain. I decided to pass on the opportunity to mention that I was, in fact, quite happy to be gay; to remind him that the young man I so foolishly chose to bring home to meet the folks, was a strapping six-footer and anything but "sissified"; or to volunteer that, notwithstanding my father's remark about my taking it up the butt, I'm basically a top.

I spoke softly, slowly, as evenly as I could manage.

"Why, you ugly old half-dead *piece* of an evil mutha-fucka. I have never in my life asked you to be proud of my gayness. I am neither proud nor ashamed of being gay. Being gay is not in and of itself an accomplishment. However," and I swallowed around a lump of soreness, "let us forget the subject of pride for just a moment" — I sniffed a wet one — "and get back to this love thing.

After all, whatever else I may be, I am your firstborn son. Your only living son. And I think it's a perfectly reasonable question to ask, so I'll ask it again, in case you missed it the first time around. Do you love me" — and I paused for a bit of dramatic effect before adding, "Father?"

Lance made no sound, save for the soft hiss of his slow, even breathing.

I waited.

Then I waited a little longer.

"Dad?" I leaned in toward my father's ear. "Dad?" Lance's only reply was his familiar, flutteringly glottal snore — a sound not unlike an old Volkswagen Beetle with serious muffler problems, taking a steep incline — the snore both David and I myself had inherited. While no longer the roar it had been in Lance's robust youth (when it resembled a Mack truck with no muffler at all), it was still a formidable sound, more than capable of filling a small hospital room.

"Perfect," I said aloud, taking my leave of Lance, the room, the snore.

Nigel looked up from a magazine as I approached. "How'd it go?" he asked.

"Oh, fine," I said. "I force-fed him three mouthfuls of baby food, then sang him to sleep."

Nigel's thick, black eyebrows rose and Nigel followed them up to a standing position. "You sang?"

"No," I said. "Could we go get some breakfast? I'd absolutely kill for a cheese omelette."

"How 'bout Anna Lee's?" Nigel said. I shot him a look — I was in no mood. "For breakfast, Captain," Nigel said, raising a shielding hand, "for breakfast. Anna Lee can burn her some grits and eggs and she'll sling it our way free-for-nothin'. Okay?" He smiled that smile.

8. Anna Lee's front room was filled with music, as before, as was very likely the usual. This time, though, the sound of the singer's voice was mine — the voice of a Johnnie Ray Rousseau some six years and a couple of heartbreaks younger. It was close enough, though, to the me standing in Anna Lee's doorway that the sharp, inner *ping!* of recognition was followed immediately by the utter excruciation I nearly always experience at hearing my own recorded voice. It was also just far enough removed that, after a moment, I could listen to it with nearly objective ears and think, "Hm, the kid's not too bad." As I followed Nigel through Anna Lee's front door and into the uninhabited front room, the voice was making its way through the last chorus of "Midnight Sun" ("but oh, my darling, always I'll remember"), a song I'd picked up from June Christy's *Something Cool* album and one of my favorite jazz tunes, to hear or sing.

"What is this?" I asked through a slightly constricted throat. "A setup?"

Nigel shook his head. "Anna Lee plays you a lot."

"Told you," Anna Lee said, striding into the room from the kitchen, wiping her hands on a dishtowel, looking like a teenager in a t-shirt and a pair of baggy floral-print weight lifter's pants. "Sure wish you'd 'a' made more than one album," she said. "I just about wore this one out, yeah." By now, she was standing face-to-face with me — or would have been, had she not been a full six inches shorter than I. "I know you must have your good reasons," she said as my disembodied singing voice hung suspended in the morning air, holding the last note of "Midnight Sun," "but you ought to be singing, baby." She wrapped her tiny hand around as much of my upper arm as she could (which wasn't very much) and gave it a little squeeze. Then she smiled as if to signal that she'd said her say. "Y'all here just to say hi," she asked, "y'all here for breakfast, or y'all here to make some hot pork sandwiches?"

"Make some what?" I said.

"Miss Anna Lee is referring to the, uh ... wild thaaang," Nigel drawled through one of those smiles of his.

"Breakfast," I said quickly. "If we're not imposing," I added.

"You couldn't if you wanted to," said Anna Lee with a little smile. "Y'all sit on down," she said, heading toward the kitchen. "How you like your eggs, Johnnie?"

"Scrambled, please," I said, smiling. There was something about this Anna Lee that kept me smiling. "Hot pork sandwiches?" I said, settling into a chair opposite Nigel at the card table near the front window where I'd met Fitty and Freen the previous afternoon.

"Kind of an 'in' thing between me and Anna Lee," Nigel said through an uncharacteristically sheepish grin. "It's from a song."

I smiled. I'm relatively sure that at least half of everything I've ever said was taken from some fifty-year-old RKO movie, some Tom Robbins novel, some Joni Mitchell song. It has long been my assertion that

if Twentieth Century-Fox had never released *All about
Eve*, I might have reached adulthood not only mute, but
utterly humorless and very likely heterosexual. "I've
been known to quote the occasional song lyric myself,"
I said.

"You don't need to quote no song lyrics, Cap," Nigel
said. "You can sing."

I laughed — a laugh hardly worthy of the word,
really. More like an outgoing sniff. "I remember when
that and a quarter'd get you on a bus."

Nigel shook his head. "Man," he said, "you just don't
know."

"Know what?"

"You got such a gift," Nigel said. From the stereo, I
heard my own years-ago voice singing "Nature Boy" a
capella, the sound of it bringing a small ache to the
bottom of my throat. "Listen to that," said Nigel. "That's
from your mother's people. None of the Rousseaus can
sing a lick. Don't you miss it? I mean, don't you miss
running that sound through your body? That music?"

I looked into my cousin's dark, liquid eyes for a
moment. The kid was so innocent, so incredibly earnest. What could he know yet, about life, about loss?
Not yet nineteen years old, not yet out of his grandmother's house.

"Nigel," I said slowly, carefully, "you're equating
music with mere sound. They're not the same. Sure, I
could sing notes, I could run sound through my body
and out my mouth. But that's not where music comes
from. You must know that. Sound," I said, pressing a
hand against my collarbone, "comes from here. Music
is from here," I moved the hand to the center of my
chest. "And here." I held my fist against my belly. "And
... farther down. And there's just—" A dull, too-familiar
ache moved from the spot beneath my palm, up into
my throat, swelled, and dissipated. "There's no music

there. There just isn't." The look on his face told me Nigel didn't understand.

"Look," I said, "it's not like I'll never open my mouth and emit notes, ever again. I'm sure I will."

"Like when?"

"Like when I'm ready," I said, and before Nigel could counter, I added, "and no, I don't know when I'll be ready, okay?"

I was still singing from the stereo. The sound of my own singing voice was beginning to annoy me. Suddenly, I wished I'd just shut up.

"I was singing the night he was killed," I said, looking at but not seeing the kitchen doorjamb over Nigel's shoulder, hardly aware that my lips moved and words tumbled past them, not sure why I was going into it all.

"Keith?" Nigel said.

I nodded. "It was a Thursday night. I was doing a one-nighter at At My Place."

"At your place?" Nigel said.

I had to smile. "At My Place is a club," I said. "Rather a nice one, as L.A. night spots go. Was one of my favorite places to play." I paused for a moment, asked myself again why I was telling this story at this time, to Nigel in Anna Lee's living room. Then I told it anyway. "Keith wanted to go. At My Place was one of the few nightclubs he could stand. He hated clubs." I felt a small tremble in my lower lip and bit down on it until the shiver passed. "But he had a bank thing to go to that night, a big cocktail thing for some of their bigger clients. He was all excited about meeting Shirley Jones — she was going to be there."

"Shirley Jones?" Nigel said. I looked up to see the grin on my cousin's face.

"His favorite movie —" I began, but then my mouth was trembling so hard I had to look away and raise my hand to cover it, to still it.

"You really want to talk about this?" Nigel asked.

I shook my head no, then continued. *"The Music Man.* His favorite movie." I closed my eyes a moment and saw myself and Keith, sprawled out on the family room sofa, smiles on our faces, watching *The Music Man* on home video. Keith's hand resting on my leg; my fingers tickling the crisp, sun-bleached hair on the back of Keith's big hand.

I felt the sour sting in my eyes and shook my head clear, opened moistened eyes. "It was a good gig," I said. "I was good that night. The combo I'd hired did not have its collective head up its collective ass, for a change. Lot of friends in the room.

"I hung out for a while afterward, which I hardly ever did. Had a drink with some fans. Flirted a little bit with this, this guy." I searched my memory for a moment, but could remember nothing of the man.

"And when I got home, just a tad late—" I fought back the onset of tears. "—no Keith. Just a rather terse message on the answering machine. From the police."

Nigel opened his mouth as if to speak, but I was ahead of him. "Wouldn't you think that a person, a person of any sensitivity, would have gotten some kind of, I don't know, premonition or something? Some kind of, of feeling, you know, that something was wrong." I bit down on my lower lip, shook my head, spoke to the tabletop. "But no. Nothing."

I hiccupped an inbreath. "Dennis has suggested that I somehow blame myself for Keith's death; that I somehow blame the fact that I was singing. But I don't really think so. It's just that — suddenly it just wasn't fun anymore, you know?"

I just sat for a moment, looking absently down toward the tabletop, my right hand still pressed against my chest, over my heart, as if saying the pledge to the flag. It wasn't until I felt the warm touch of Nigel's fingertips on the back of my left hand that I realized that that hand was clenched in a tight fist. My fingers uncurled as Nigel rested his palm over the back of my hand.

"I'm real sorry," Nigel said.

"Yeah," I said, not looking up.

9.

Lance in his underwear, walking. Lance's white Fruit of the Loom briefs full of Lance, bulging low and lumpy in front, the back full of Lance's high-set, meaty behind. A little tuft of nappy, light brown hair at the small of his back, just above the waistband of those shorts. Lance's big ass shifting beneath the white cloth as he walks.

Wanting to touch that ass, to fall face-first into the white-cloth-covered mounds of ass-muscle, wanting to kiss it.

View from the open bathroom doorway. Lance standing at the toilet. Young, barely thirty, handsome and nearly naked. Heavy shoulders and deep, fuzzy chest. Big, toast brown dick and balls hanging heavy as ripe fruit over the top of his underpants, pissing a thick stream into the water. All at eye level and surprisingly, wonderfully in close-up, as if the eye were a zoom lens.

Wanting to cross the threshold, to enter the room. Wanting to reach hands out and hold the dick, cup the balls, wet both hands and face with piss. Lance's. Father's.

Lance's head turning, his brow frowning, upper lip curling, exposing white, straight teeth. Lance saying,

"What are you lookin' at?" Lance staring back, his face growing ugly with anger. "Junie?" he says, his voice high, a woman's voice.

"Junie?" I awoke at the touch of Aunt Lucille's hand on my arm; my eyes clicked open, and I let out a little noise. The nose-pinching hospital smell brought me quickly back to the tiny room where my father lay drawn and still beneath the plastic tent.

I had a hard-on. Jesus, I thought — I am not a well woman.

"You all right, baby?" Lucille asked, her hand curling around my forearm.

"I'm fine," I said, crossing my legs with some difficulty. "I just nodded off for a minute," I added, choosing to omit the fact that in that minute I'd enjoyed a brief one-reel triple-X movie starring thirty-year-old images of my now-comatose father. "Haven't slept through the night in a solid year, but I will take the occasional catnap sitting up in an uncomfortable plastic chair in a hospital room." I did a big, vaudevillian shoulder shrug. "Go figure."

"Poor child," Aunt Lucille said, stroking the back of my hand with her soft, warm palm. She'd arrived a couple of hours before, driven by Nigel, who had gone to fetch his grandmother immediately upon learning of Lance's turn for the worse, the old man having fallen into a coma while I'd been making short work of a better-than-average bacon-and-eggs breakfast at Anna Lee's. As I was passing the front desk, not feeling the need to check in, feeling rather like a "regular," the young desk nurse called out, "He in a coma." Her words had stopped me like a Plexiglas wall. "Yo' daddy," she said, as if I might imagine she was referring to someone else — the pope, the president, Michael Jackson. "He in a coma."

I had sat alone until Lucille's arrival, eyes shut, breathing slowly, attempting a calm, meditative state, falling somewhat short of that. She'd arrived on Nigel's arm, pristine white running shoes on her feet, repeating, "Oh, my Lord" and "Lord have mercy today." Nigel deposited his grandmother and retreated. "I be back for y'all later," he said, and left for parts unknown, leaving Lucille and me to sit side by side for the long afternoon; seldom speaking ("Can I get you anything?" I asked. "No, thank you, cher," she said); Lucille mumbling prayers (the odd "sweet Lord" or "dear Father" slipping from between her lips); and me doing my best to meditate: breathing slowly in, even more slowly out, concentrating only on the breath itself. It was both a largely vain attempt at relaxation and an entirely vain attempt to make time collapse like an old telescope, bringing Nigel and the car back to take me away from my father's dying-room, if only for a while.

"Lord, I wish things coulda' been better between you and your daddy," Lucille said, out of nowhere in particular.

And I thought: Yeah, and if wishes were Porsches, then beggars would ride. But I didn't say anything.

"You know, your daddy loves you," she added.

Big eye-roll from me. "Yeah, right."

"What?" Lucille leaned in, as if slightly deaf.

"Nothing," I said. I was immediately sorry I'd allowed the words out. I knew I was in danger of hurting Lucille, and there was no reason for that. I felt the stinging slap of Lucille's ring-heavy hand on my arm.

"What you talkin' about, boy?" My aunt turned to me, head cocked, one eyebrow raised high, looking at me as if I'd just mistaken diamonds for dog shit.

I shrugged, rubbing the smarting spot on my arm. "Never mind," I said. "I didn't mean that."

"Never mind, my foot," Lucille said. Then she glanced toward the plastic-tented bed where her brother lay and lowered her voice to an abrasive whisper, as if raising her voice might disturb Lance's sleep. "Don't be rolling your eyes, trying to say your daddy don't love you, and then give me all this 'Never mind, I didn't mean it.'" She gave a little nod of her head and said, "Of course he loves you. He's your daddy."

I took a deep breath; let it out; considered a hasty retreat ("Yes, of course, you're right — I'm just upset"), but changed my mind. If we were going to talk about this, then we might as well just talk about it.

"Has he ever told you he loved me?" I asked, all too rhetorically. "Just, like, mention it in passing? Did he ever say, you know, that firstborn son of mine is on the strange side, but I can't help but love his black ass? Did he?"

"Now, you know your daddy ain't never been the kind to talk like that," Lucille said softly, averting her eyes from mine.

"And as we all know, he never asked me to come here. And didn't want to see me once I got here."

Lucille did not respond.

"So, with all due respect, ma'am," I said, slipping into Elvis-ese, "I don't believe you know what you're talking about." I swiveled in my seat to face my aunt, who looked rather as if she'd been slapped, her eyes wide, lips agape. "I know," I said. "I knew it at ten years old and I sure as shit know it now, excuse my French." Lucille lifted a forefinger and started to speak, but I rolled on ahead. "I'm sure he loved me when I was a baby and probably when I was a little kid — I mean, after all, he was my father and I was his firstborn. But it wasn't me he loved, because I hadn't actually become me yet. He loved the normal little boy he thought I was, that it never would have occurred to him I wasn't.

"But the older I got, the more me I became. And the more me I became, the less he loved me. And by that time, he had—" I hiccupped a mouthful of air, swallowed back the little sore lump in my throat. "By that time, there was David, there was my little brother David, who was everything my father wanted in a son, where I was nothing he wanted. God," I said, turning away, facing the oxygen tent again, "I can't believe I'm going over this territory again."

"Junie," Lucille attempted, but I wasn't finished yet.

"And if there was the smallest..." I made a fluttery gesture in the air with my hands, searching for a word. "...modicum of love left for me — let's face it, folks — it died with David. And for years, I was able to tell myself I didn't care. Feh! Who needs him?

"But then I get your call, out of the blue. And like a fool, I dragged my tired, hate-to-fly butt all the way out here, hoping, just hoping that finally, flat on his back, knocking on heaven's door, Lance Rousseau might be able to look at me and say, 'I love you, Son. I don't understand you, but I do love you.'

"But he didn't. He couldn't. He doesn't." I sat for a moment, staring through the oxygen tent at the opposite wall.

"Child," Lucille said softly, "you really believe that?"

"I know it," I said.

I felt Lucille's warm, cushioned hand on my shoulder, felt my tightened deltoid muscle relax just slightly under her touch. "Well," she said, her voice barely audible, "I think you're wrong. I think you got love all mixed up with approve. Your father don't approve of the way you live, but that don't mean he don't love you. Lord, Junie — parents love their children. They can't help it. That's what the Lord put us here for — to love our children and make them miserable." After a moment, she added, "That was a joke."

"I'm sorry," I said. "I misplaced my sense of humor a good while ago."

"Your daddy loves you," Lucille said. "This I know."

I suppressed the urge to add, "For the Bible tells me so," and we sat together in silence again, as we had for most of the day. Less than a minute later, I turned at the sound of a wet sniff. Lucille, a fisted handkerchief against her mouth, wept, tears falling down her plump brown cheeks and onto her knuckles.

"On the other hand," she said, "maybe I'm full of shit." She sniffed again and added, "Excuse my French."

By the time Nigel came and taxied Aunt Lucille and me back to the house, I wanted nothing so much as a good, hard Nautilus workout, followed by half an hour in a steaming-hot jacuzzi. It had been three days since I'd last faced a Nautilus double-chest machine, which is just about my limit before the onset of serious gym withdrawal. Being Lord-knows-how-many miles from a decent health club, I settled for the set of Sears plastic-covered concrete weights living in Nigel's room. When, immediately upon entering Aunt Lucille's house, I asked Nigel's permission to use his weight set, the boy showed the extreme good taste not to question why a man might leave his father's deathbed with the barely controlled urge to execute sets of barbell curls to temporary muscular failure. He simply said, "No prob, Captain. Need a spotter?"

We had barely completed two sets of bench presses apiece before the air in Nigel's room had grown thick with humidity and pungent with our collective bodily funks. Nigel's entire set of weights was only 200 pounds, but with super-slow repetitions (slow count of ten up, slow count of five down) I was able to achieve a satisfactory "pump," that warm, rapid influx of blood into worked muscle that Arnold Schwartzenegger used to compare favorably with orgasm (an opinion I have never shared), and which made me feel as if my pectoral muscles might rip my sweat-soaked t-shirt off me, as if I were the Incredible Hulk. There was something about this animal sensation, this hot, prickly body rush, that could often bring me out, or at least nearer the murky surface, of a depression, where an hour lying flat on my back in Savasana (the yoga position also known as "the Corpse"), breathing deeply, or even a Billie Holiday tape on the Walkman, might not.

Nigel lay prone on the weight bench, wearing only a pair of sawed-off blue jeans hanging precariously low against his hipbones, and an overcoat of sweat that accentuated the swollen muscles of his chest and arms as he wrapped his fingers around the weight bar. Standing at the head of the bench, hands cupped under the bar, my groin a scant few inches from my cousin's face, it occurred to me how reminiscent was my current situation of any number of scenes in any number of triple-X all-male videos with titles like *Black Load, Black Champs,* and *Forbidden Black Fantasies.* The thought was making the trip from my head to the crotch of my UCLA gym shorts (where my dick, deprived of the blood pumped into my pecs and triceps, sat atop my ball sac, reduced to the size of a small toadstool), and was very nearly there (old Snarfle stirred just a bit, as if he could hear the train in the distance), when Nigel sat up and said, without actually looking back at me, "Can I ask you something?"

"Ask, I said.

Nigel swiveled around on the bench, throwing one leg over and straddling it, and said, "You dating anybody?"

I suddenly had to sit down. It was only a few steps to Nigel's bed; I took them and sat, feeling leaden. I said, "What on earth makes you ask a thing like that?"

Nigel did a little shrug. "I was wondering. If it's none of my damn business, just say so."

My initial inclination was to just say so and try to get back into a nice, uncomplicated set of bench presses. But my cousin had already learned more about the darker nights of my little soul over the past two days than anybody this side of my therapist. What would be the point of holding back at this stage of the game?

"Toss me a towel," I said. I stalled a moment by removing my sweat-drenched t-shirt and blotting my forehead, chest, and armpits with a small, rather threadbare towel. "I have dated," I said, and then added, "a little. And it was..." Lord, how do I begin to describe it? "...not wonderful."

Nigel raised an eyebrow at me. "Not wonderful?"

My stomach tightened. I wanted nothing so much as to backpedal and invoke the none-of-your-damn-business clause. I didn't — damned if I know why. "It was five, six months before I could even think about seeing anybody. I just couldn't. For the first couple of months, it was as if my genitals had fallen off. I didn't even seem to have any discernible desires. Men didn't even appeal to me. To the extent that there was anything to sublimate, I worked it off in the gym. Free weights, machines, aerobics, yoga — I was in the gym five and six times a week. I got into the best shape of my life, guys were tossing themselves at me like flies against a windshield, and I just didn't care, didn't want any. I didn't even beat off. Nothing."

"But you did go out," Nigel said, leaning his arms against the weight bar, his chin against his arms.

I nodded. "Finally. Started about four months ago."

Danny, the half-Cherokee would-be rock star with arrow-straight shoulder-length hair and a flaming Fender Stratocaster guitar tattooed on his right arm, who let me know what he wanted with one raised eyebrow and a nasty little smile in the showers at the gym. Hailed from a little backwater even smaller than the one I currently sat in, just outside Mobile, Alabama. Talked so naughty in that drawl of his, my toes curled into fists.

Curtis, the big-dicked cock-sucking surfer I picked up hitching toward Venice Beach, who tasted like salt and smelled like baby oil, and who called me "Dude," even while we made love in the narrow bed of the mobile home he lived in ("Aw, yeah, fuck me, Dude!"). And whose penis was one of the prettiest I'd ever seen — long and fat-headed, cherry pink and apple blossom white.

"Meet anybody special?" Nigel asked.

"No," I said. "Not really."

Neil, the pretty-faced blond hairdresser-slash-aerobics instructor from Studio City I met at the Sunday beer bust at the Mother Lode, with a tummy you could wash lingerie on and a tongue that did everything but play "Flight of the Bumblebee" on my nipples.

"Date anybody more than once?" asked Nigel.

I thought a moment.

Deryck. The semisweet-chocolate-colored ex-dancer. Deryck who walked right up to me on Wilshire Boulevard in front of Neiman Marcus in Beverly Hills on a big, fat Saturday morning in broad daylight and said, "Man, you are lookin' some kinda good," like we were old lovers or something. Deryck of the impossibly high, round dancer's ass and a haircut much like Nigel's, who squired me into Neiman's and proceeded to buy me lunch.

I saw him more than once, didn't I? Or did I just tell him I would as I accepted his telephone number? And what was the point of the question, anyway?

"What's the difference?" I asked Nigel, suddenly feeling like I was sitting in the midst of a fifty-minute hour in Dennis's big leather armchair.

Nigel shrugged. "I was just wondering if maybe it wasn't time you got back in the game, that's all."

"There is no formal timetable for grief," I said. Just who does this little punk think he is, anyway?

"Sounds like something your therapist told you," he said.

"Well," I said, growing more irritated by the second, "aren't we just the little expert on everything."

Nigel raised a protecting palm and said, "Whoa, Cap."

"Just what are you getting at, here?" I said, my voice rising in volume and pitch. "I've dated. I've had sex. All right, Doctor? Did I enjoy it? Pretty much. Did any one event or the sum total of it hold a candle to making love just once with the man I loved for ten years? Fuck no!"

"Of course not," Nigel said, hand still raised, his voice calm and many decibel levels below my own. He paused long enough for one long breath, in and out, then added, "I'm just wondering if any man you haven't loved for ten years is going to have a chance, that's all."

"You know something, little boy? You don't know what the fuck you're talking about." I was shouting by this time, jabbing a finger at the air between Nigel and me, fairly trembling with what I assumed was anger. "I fell in love with Keith Keller while you were still learning your times tables. After you've loved somebody ten years — cooked his dinners and packed his lunches and sucked his dick and taken his temperature and breathed his goddamn morning breath for ten fuckin' years of your life. And then lose that — just have that taken away from you for no good reason. Then you come back and tell me how easy it is for you to get back in the goddamn game."

"Aw, Jesus, Cap," Nigel said, rising from the bench and moving toward me. "What we got here," he said, a little smile curling his lips, "is a failure to communicate." He sat next to me on the bed, rested a damp palm on my equally humid knee. "All I was trying to say is, you don't want to be so busy missing Keith, remembering how much you loved him, that you won't even recognize love the next time you see it. See?" He stroked long, warm ovals up and down my knee with his hand. "'Cause right now," he said, "I don't think you'd know love if it was sittin' on your face, singin' 'How High the Moon.'"

"Oh, I get it now," I said, moving my knee out from under Nigel's hand. "This isn't about how many guys I've dated or whether I've met anybody special or if I'll ever love anybody ever again. This is about how I don't think it's such a hot idea to sixty-nine with you all over this little backwater. Isn't it?"

Nigel stood up and took a step away from me. "Is that what you think?" His mouth opened and shut a couple of times, and then he finally said, "You know something? Fuck you."

"Oh, that's very mature," I said.

"I gotta go," he said, turned, and fairly marched from the room.

Leaving me alone with 200 pounds of barbell and my pumped-up pectorals. And the increasingly insistent, increasingly disturbing thought that the kid might just be right.

11. "Is Nigel here?" I stood in the doorway of Anna Lee's house, dabbing at my sweat-dripping face and neck with my handkerchief in a gesture of utter futility, having walked the mile or so from Aunt Lucille's to Anna Lee's in a humid midday heat the likes of which neither mad dog nor Englishman would brave. My question was largely rhetorical: the Blue Bomb was nowhere to be seen, and I knew wherever he'd gone, Nigel had taken the car.

"No," said Anna Lee, a little smile on her lips. She tilted her head to one side, her dreadlocks shifting. "Did you lose him?"

"Sort of," I said, still dabbing. "We had ... well, we sort of..."

"Why don't you come in the house," Anna Lee said, taking me by a clammy hand and pulling me indoors. "You're letting all kinds of hot air in," she added, closing the door behind me, "and we sure don't need none of that."

"We had kind of an argument," I finally finished.

"Lord, child!" I turned toward the sound of a newly familiar voice (a voice soft yet husky, like silk tearing), to see Mr. Freen and Mr. Fitty seated at the card table where I had first encountered them the day before, playing cards in their hands and on the table between them. "What you doin' out in this heat, baby?" asked Freen.

"Let me get you some water," Anna Lee offered before I could answer him, touching me softly on one damp shoulder.

"Ought to get that wet shirt offa you too," added Freen.

"I just bet you want him outta that shirt," said Fitty.

"Aw, shut up, Fitty," said Freen. "Ain't nobody said nothin' to you, no-way."

"I was looking for Nigel," I said.

"He ain't here," said Freen.

"The boy can see that, fool," Fitty said.

"Thought I done told you to shut the fuck up."

"You thought? You thought you could play gin, too, muthafucka, but you see I'm kickin' your black ass from here to Dog Town."

Anna Lee emerged from the kitchen carrying a large tumbler of ice water.

"Both of y'all shut up, please," she said, handing me the glass.

"Didn't feel like playin' gin, no-way." Freen leaned his toothless black face in closer to Fitty's pale, pointed one. "Rather be kickin' your ol' long, hangin'-way-down, almost-white butt all over the boneyard. 'Cause you know I'll domino you to death."

"Dominoes?" Fitty's voice shot up a good octave and a third. "I'm whippin' you in gin and I'll whip you in dominoes, too, muthafucka."

"Anna Lee," Freen called as if Anna Lee were across the road rather than standing at his elbow. "Anna Lee, get them dominoes, darlin', 'cause we goin' down to the boneyard today. Matter of fact," he said, wagging a long index finger in my direction, "sit on down, boy. Let's play us some teams. You be my partner. Move out that chair, Fitty," he said, waving a hand in Mr. Fitty's direction as if he were a bothersome dragonfly. "Anna Lee, you partner Fitty."

"Teams?" Fitty said, all but singing the word on three long notes. "You just lookin' for a excuse for losin'. 'Wadn't *my* fault. Couldn't he'p it. It was my partner.'"

"You so fulla shit," Freen said, wagging his head from side to side, "you sho' ought to be more brown. We gots four peoples in here, four peoples ought to play, thass all."

I said, "I'm not much of a domino player, I'm afraid." Which is true. I've never been much of a strategist, my mind tends to wander, and I'm not much good at remembering what's been played. Which makes me a so-so card player — the outstanding feature of my bridge playing is the skillful way I refill the drinks when I'm dummy — and an equally so-so domino player.

Freen smiled a dark, toothless grin as Anna Lee returned to the table with the small wooden box of domino pieces. "That's all right, son," he said. "I'm good enough for both of us."

■

Freen slid the double-five domino into place with a long-fingered, knotty-knuckled ebony black hand. He cocked his head to one side, made a purse-lipped little face, and said, "Why, I do believe that's twenty-five. Score that li'l ol' twenty-five-ski, Junie. Man alive, twenty-five. How bad we beatin' this pretty little lady and this ugly ol' Cajun now, Junie?" He leaned across the table toward me and the pad of paper on which I was keeping score. I drew five little tick marks representing the twenty-five points, did a quick count, and said, "We've got two hundred and ten, to their one hundred and five."

Freen smiled and said, "We playin' for forty, Shorty."

"Don't mean shit," Mr. Fitty said. He sat to my left, three ivory dominoes cupped in his palm. "Game ain't hardly over just 'cause you done got some little piddly-shit twenty-five. Ain't over 'til the fat lady *sangs*."

Freen curved a hand around one ear and said, "Why, I do believes I can hear her tunin' up right now. Sprayin' her big-ol' th'oat, gettin' ready to wail." He treated me to a big, exaggerated wink. "This game half bullshit," he said in a stage whisper. "Win or lose, you gots to keep bullshittin'."

Anna Lee rapped her knuckles against the tabletop, signaling that she was unable to play.

"You knockin'?" Fitty said.

"Sho' sounded like it to me," Freen said through a grin.

I didn't have to pass, but I couldn't score either. I pushed the domino into place. "I can't score," I said with a little shrug of my shoulders.

"Thass all right, baby," Freen said. "Know why? 'Cause the name of this game is domino. And I'm set to domino, yeah." He danced one ivory domino between his thumb and finger, its plain off-white back to me. "This here's the dominoin' bone, right here."

Fitty sat quietly contemplating the bones on the table, then the bones in his hand, then the ones on the table.

Freen said, a bit louder than absolutely necessary, "You gon' play this year, man, or what?"

"Ahma play 'Chopsticks' upside yo' head, you don't shut up and let me think."

Freen widened his pink-cornered eyes, threw up his hands in mock surrender. "Yes, sir, think all you want. Don't mean shit, 'cause I got the dominoin' bone right here." He laughed one of his long *HEEEE-hee-hee* laughs, his shoulders rising up toward his ears. He sniffed, picked at the corner of one eye with his finger, looked across the table at me for a moment, and said, "Boy, you sho' do favor yo' daddy as a young man. You small like yo' mama, but you built just like L.J. Just as handsome, too," he added, nudging my leg with his foot, a foot clad only in an old black sock, a foot which took its own sweet time traveling down my shin and onto the top of my sneakered foot.

"Take yo' stinkin' foot offa that boy," Fitty said, not looking up from the dominoes. "Old sissy-man."

"How you know where my foot is?" Freen demanded, as he slid his foot off mine.

"I been known you since this boy wasn't nothin' but his daddy hitchin' his pants up, thass how I know."

"You knew my father when he was young," I said, not exactly a question, since I knew he had.

"Knew your mama, too," Freen said. "Since they's babies."

"What were they like?" I asked. "As kids, I mean. Teenagers." I had never seen so much as a photograph of either of my parents as children. So far as I knew, none existed. I hoped this funny old man's memory might be able to paint me a yearbook picture of them.

"We gonna play dominoes or what?" Fitty said.

"You ready to play?" Freen asked.

"In a minute."

"Then shut the fuck up, then," Freen said. Then, to me, "Thing I remember best about yo' daddy as a young, young man, sixteen, seventeen years old — between the time he quit the high school and the time he went off to Korea — was his walk. Had this bad-ass, sexy walk, like to drive the little girls crazy." He leaned in toward me. "Like to drive me crazy, too. Had that high butt like you got, and them big-ol' arms like you got. Like to roll his shirt sleeves way up, show 'em off. When he'd be walkin' toward the rice fields down in Dog Town to work, he be walkin' that walk of his: slow, like he didn't really have to go to no work, no-way.

"Walked right from the crotch," he said. "Groin first, like he was ready to fuck the whole world."

"Tried to fuck most of it," Fitty said, never looking away from the table, "if I remember right."

"Womanizer?" I said, hardly surprised.

"Lord, ha' mercy," Freen said. "Look like that boy was always on the hard. Was stickin' that thang ev'ry-where." The old man chuckled. "Your grammaw Eudora had this cow—"

"Cow?"

"I guess you city boys don't know 'bout that," Fitty said, still staring down the dominoes.

"I do not believe this conversation," said Anna Lee, getting up from the table and heading toward the kitchen. "Y'all want a Coke or something?"

"Sebb'm-Up," Fitty said.

"Not for me," said Freen.

"No, thank you," I said, detecting a small crack in my voice.

"Ahma tell you a li'l secret," Freen whispered across the table. He leaned over until his sunken chest nearly brushed the tops of the dominoes on the table. "I had me a little piece of L.J. myself."

"You what?" I said, my voice a squeak.

"You a damn lie," Fitty said, finally looking up.

"If I'm lyin' I'm flyin'," Freen said, drawing an X across his chest with an index finger.

"You shouldn't be telling this boy lies about his daddy. God'll punish you, yeah."

"You're not kidding, are you?" I said, suddenly fascinated (and just a wee bit titillated) by the idea of a teenage Lance Rousseau, hormones running amuck, engaging in — in what? "What did you," I stammered, "what did he..."

"I done tol' you, he was stickin' his big-ol' thing ev'rywhere he *thought* it'd fit. Don't mean nothin'. Like the ol' song say," and the old man began to sing, largely on one note and in no discernible key:

> *Woke up this mornin'*
> *my bizniss in my hand*
> *Woke up this mornin'*
> *got my bizniss in my hand*
> *Can't find no woman*
> *Bring me a sissy man.*

"Lord ha' mercy," Anna Lee said, emerging from the kitchen with a bottle of 7-Up in one hand and a can of Caffeine-free Diet Coke in the other. "If you love me, Mr. Freen, please don't sing."

I fought back a laugh, but Mr. Fitty didn't bother. He snickered through his remaining teeth as he finally placed a domino on the table. "Thass twunny," he said, still laughing.

"What?" Freen studied the table quickly.

"Twunny," Fitty repeated. "Right on the money, Bugs Bunny."

"Looks like twenty from here," Anna Lee said as she and Fitty gave each other "five," right palm sliding across right palm.

"Don't mean shit," Freen said, laying down a domino but not scoring any points. "This the dominoin' bone, anyhow," he said, rapping his fingernail on the back of his last domino.

"Well, well, well," I said, smiling in amused surprise at this little piece of family history. "You and the Lance. What will be next?"

"Oh, yeah," Freen said with a little head nod. "He let me have my way. Of course, he kicked my ass afterwards."

"He what?" I suppose this should not have surprised me, but it did.

Freen made a dismissing hand gesture and said, "Made him feel better, I guess. More like the man. 'Sides, it was worth a ass-kickin', far as I was concerned. That boy was some kinda *tasty.*"

"Man, what you tryin' to do?" Fitty said, making a sour face and clutching at his concave belly. "Make me puke?"

"Aw, git over yourself," Freen said, executing a finger snap involving his entire right arm and shoulder. "Oh, yeah. Mr. L.J. was somethin' else. Coulda had any girl who passed him on the street. So when he up and married that big-ol' homely gal, ev'rybody knew it was 'cause he *had* to."

"Homely?" I said. "My mom?"

Freen made a face at me and said, "Not yo' mama, child."

"Freen," Fitty tried to interrupt.

"Annie-Belle," Freen said.

"Freen," Fitty tried again.

"His *first* wife," said Freen.

"Dammit, Freen!"

"I done played, you ugly pink-eyed, redheaded muthafucka, it's Anna Lee's turn!"

"My father had a first wife?"

Freen's toothless mouth swung open like an old outhouse door. "Aw, shit," he said. "I forgot."

"You stupid-ass ol' fool!" Fitty said, slamming his two remaining dominoes down onto the table, making a sound like a cap pistol.

"I said I forgot," Freen said, half plea, half challenge. "I'm sorry."

"What?" Anna Lee said. "What y'all talking about?"

"Wasn't neither one of L.J.'s children supposed to know about Annie-Belle," Fitty said. "When L.J. married Clara Jane, he said that part of his life was over, wasn't no use talkin' about it." He turned toward Freen (whose facial expression made me think of constipation) and said, "Most people been able to keep they big mouth shut, 'til now."

"I said I's sorry," Freen said, his lips barely moving.

"Well?" I said, hungry for as much information as I could squeeze out of the two old men at the table about this chapter in my father's life. "You might as well tell me now."

Fitty and Freen looked first at each other, then at me, then at each other again. Finally, Fitty said, "Ain't all that much to tell."

"So?" I said. "Tell, already."

"You may as well finish up," Fitty said to Freen, then added, "y'ol' blabbermouth fool."

Freen said, "You kiss my en*tire* ass, Fitty, hear me?" Then turned to me and said, "L.J. did right by Annie-Belle. She got pregnant and he married her. She died birthin' the baby; L.J. went to Korea. When he got back, he married Clara Jane. Pretty little thing with her hair all up in plaits, big-ol' deep dimples in her face, just like you got." He shrugged his narrow shoulders. "Thass it."

"'Thass it,'" Fitty mocked Freen with a pinched little voice and a mouth-twisting face. "That ain't it and you know it. Your daddy sent money to care for Annie-Belle's child from his army pay, and didn't stop sending money 'til Andrew died."

It was an aspect of my father I had not considered, certainly not recently. Here was a man who, while perhaps lacking a great capacity for affection, was certainly — even in his early twenties — not without a certain sense of duty, of what I've heard my Louisiana relatives call "do-right."

And then it hit me.

Andrew.

Adrenaline shot through me and my heart rate picked up speed.

"Andrew? You don't mean my cousin Andrew, who used to live with Great-Aunt Hattie?"

"Wasn't none o' yo' cousin," Fitty said softly. "Was yo' brothuh. Half brother, anyhow."

"Shit a meat-axe." No wonder Lance had dragged David and me, literally kicking and screaming, to Great-Aunt Hattie's house at least once every Louisiana visit, commanding us to "Say hi to your cousin," as if our alleged cousin understood. "Wait a minute," I said. "If Cousin Andrew was actually my half brother Andrew, who the hell was Great-Aunt Hattie?"

"Annie-Belle's mama," Freen said, picking up Fitty's 7-Up and sipping noisily from it. "Wasn't no kinda kin to you," he said, then cocked his head to one side, glanced upward, and added, "least, I don't think so. You know, just about everybody round here kin to each other some kinda way, you go back far enough."

"Put down my soda, niggah," Fitty said. Freen all but dropped the bottle to the table.

"Hattie loved her some L.J.," Freen said. "Never thought Annie-Belle would catch her a pretty man like him, with her *ugly* self. Took care of his child to his last day."

"Shit a meat-axe," I repeated. My father, my mother, my entire family — and the rest of St. Charles, to boot — had kept my father's first marriage a secret from me. My dead cousin was my dead brother and my great-aunt Hattie wasn't my great-aunt at all. Mostly to myself, I said, "My sister, my daughter, my sister, my daughter. When did my life become a Roman Polanski film?"

"Who?" Fitty and Freen asked in stereo.

"Never mind."

Freen reached across the table and touched my arm with the tips of his fingers. "Don't tell Lucille I told," he said. "She like to come down here and kick my ass."

I gave his soft, smooth hand a little squeeze and said, "I won't tell."

"Nigel," Anna Lee said, as if answering a question. I looked up and toward the front door, where Nigel stood, having come in without knocking (apparently his habit).

"How you doin', Anna Lee," he said, walking toward the table. "Mr. Fitty." He nodded first toward the pale old man and then the dark one. "Mr. Freen." The two old men returned Nigel's greeting. Nigel came to stand at the corner of the table nearest my chair and rested his fingertips on the table.

"I'm sorry, Cap," he said. "I was out of line."

"No," I said, "I'm sorry." I offered my right hand. "Friends?" Nigel took my hand in his and held it tight for a moment.

"Friends," he said, with a sheepish little-boy grin. "Come on," he gestured with his head toward the door, "I'll take you back to the house."

"Not now, you ain't," Freen announced, waving one small ivory game piece. "I'm about to domino!"

12.

I couldn't seem to get to sleep that night. Nigel had stayed up with me through "The Tonight Show" before sleep got the better of him and he left me to endure most of a truly mediocre B-Western alone, determined to get to sleep without chemical assistance even if I had to exhaust every nerve in my body to get there. The air in the back bedroom was typically warm and moist, my body was tacky with sweat, and my head buzzed like old electrical wiring. I heard Lance ordering me from his hospital room over and over in an annoying mental tape loop. Nigel's face — grinning, talking, executing that Groucho Marxist eyebrow wiggle — flashed behind my eyes like a slide presentation. Ella sang the same four bars of the scat break from "How High the Moon" again and again until I seriously feared for what was left of my sanity.

At some point I fell asleep. I know, because the Dream came.

I floated toward the gurney as usual, but for the first time I could recall, I stopped myself before reaching the thing, willing myself to awaken, breathless and trembling.

And then I slept again.

And again, dreamed of Keith. But this dream was different.

We lay naked together, Keith and I, in the big oak four-poster bed we'd shared for a decade. But the Keith who lay on top of me, my face in his big hands, covering my mouth with his, wasn't the Keith I'd last seen alive just over twelve months earlier; but the Keith Keller with whom I had fallen in love a decade before: a muscular, clean-shaven man barely into his mid-twenties. And I thought,

This is a dream.

And, as often happens in dreams, it seemed as if every one of my senses had been accounted for: the room was full of Keith's smell, of the way Keith had smelled all those years ago: sweat and Certs and Brut after-shave. And when I reached down his back, I touched warm skin and hair and firm, thick muscle. He looked down at me and smiled the smile that won me, the smile that exhibited his short, even teeth, created fan pleats at the corners of his eyes, and made him the most handsome he ever looked.

"Oh, God," I said aloud. "This is a dream, isn't it?" And Keith said, "What difference does it make?" And I wrapped myself around him, gathering as much of his big-muscled body into my arms as I could hold, and felt his lips and tasted his tongue. I counted the moles on his back and yanked at a handful of his hair. And his breath was sweet in my face, his armpit moist and pungent to my lips and nostrils, and his hands stroked my sides, pinched my nipples, kneaded my ass. And as I reached for his hard, slightly right-veering, sweetly familiar dick with my fingers,

I woke up. Entangled in my sheets, wet and funky with my own sweat, my dick throbbing like a sore.

I pushed my face into a pillow to muffle the noise and cried until my throat rasped and the back of my head pounded as if I were being hit with a mallet again and again.

By the moonlight edging in around the window shades, I made my way to the bathroom on Gumby legs, wet a washcloth with cool water, and rubbed my face and neck with it. Standing damp and naked on a hot night on a cool linoleum floor, unable to control the trembling that seemed to begin at the core of me and radiate out to my arms and legs, I knew all too clearly what I wanted to do. And I knew just as clearly that I shouldn't. I stood and trembled and clutched the wet washcloth, and told myself I shouldn't.

There wasn't much light, and my contact lenses were out. And the bathroom mirror was old and rusty and distorting even in the brightest light of morning. So the man who looked back at me from the other side of that mirror was blurred, indistinct, ghostly. I could barely see his lips, but his voice was clear as he said, "Fuck 'shouldn't.'"

■

Nigel raised himself up on one elbow as I opened his bedroom door and stepped in. "Johnnie," he said. He pushed himself back toward the wall as I approached his bed, and without so much as a "May I," I slipped in beside him.

"Do you think such close physical proximity is wise?" he whispered.

"Shut up and hold me," I said.

He said, "Anything for you, Cap."

■

In the relative privacy of Nigel's bedroom, with the help of a small bottle of personal lubricant and several

Trojan-brand lubricated latex condoms which Nigel
had secreted in the back corner of his sock drawer, my
cousin and I explored each other like pioneers survey-
ing brave new worlds. My cousin's body was terra nova
and I was Columbus, Admiral Perry, both Stanley and
Livingstone ("Dr. Perineum, I presume?"). And my
cousin, Nigel Walker, boldly went where no eighteen-
year-old boy had gone before.

He climbed my every mountain, and I may or may
not have heard a yodel, I can't be sure. I slid smiling
into his valley.

We sixty-nined lying in a crooked diagonal across
Nigel's bed, traded blow jobs up on our knees on Nigel's
bed, and then traded funky-tasting tongue, standing
up, leaning against the wall next to Nigel's bed, before
taking a break for a glass of water. By the light of the
open Frigidaire, I grinned to watch Nigel's amazing
eighteen-year-old dick raise its head toward the ceiling
as he made audible short work of first one, then another
tumbler of Sparkletts water. I took hold of that boner
and pulled Nigel toward me.

I kissed him in the kitchen.

I sucked him in the hall.

I got some on my fingers and I wiped it on the wall.

He diddled me like a doggie on the bedroom floor. I
rode him like a bronze buckaroo — Nigel barely hanging
on to the edge of the bed, me standing up, tall in the
saddle, yippie-yi-o-ky-ay.

"Do you even *know* 'How High the Moon'?" I asked,
my lips in full contact with my cousin's ear.

He knew it.

Later, I lay on my side, tucked back-to-front against
the hot and moist and hard that was my cousin Nigel,
succumbing to the sweet, heavy postorgasmic-utter-
exhaustion-near-sleep and the soft electric tickle of
Nigel's fingertips tracing figure eights along my triceps.

And Nigel said, "When did you first realize you were queer?"

I smiled. "Why do you ask?"

I felt Nigel's shrug. "I donno. Just came to my mind." He nudged me with a knee. "So when?"

"Well, as soon as I found out there was such a word as 'homosexual,'" I said. "Yep, that's me all right. No hesitation. I was maybe, twelve?" I turned over onto my back; Nigel rested a hand on my belly. "But I'm sure I was queer long before that. I mean, I had an erotic dream about Ricky Nelson when I was in kindergarten."

"Ricky Nelson?" Nigel raised up on one elbow. "Like Ozzie and Harriet? Like the irrepressible Ricky?"

"The very one," I admitted. "I dreamed I was watching television, and Ricky was singing 'Traveling Man.' I don't know if you ever noticed this, but the sight of Ricky Nelson's lips forming the words 'pretty Polynesian baby,' is one of the most erotic visuals in entertainment history."

"Can't say as I've ever noticed that," said Nigel.

"Pity. Anyway, in this dream, all of a sudden Ricky's in the nude, butt-ass naked, and I'm seeing him from the back. And he's rocking from side to side and he's got this ass. I mean this incredible ass." I felt my dick plump at the memory of a thirty-year-old dream of a years-dead teen idol. "Needless to say, 'Traveling Man' is something of a special song for me. And then, in the fourth grade, I fell madly in love with Joel Brechtschneider. This flawless little blond boy. I'm afraid I had something of a blond fetish for many years after that. However" — I turned toward Nigel and slurped his nearest nipple — "I got over it. And how about you? When did it first occur to you that you were, as you say, enchanted?"

Nigel didn't speak immediately. He turned over onto his back and studied the ceiling fan for a long moment.

Finally, he said, "When I was six years old, I developed a major crush on my cousin Junie."

Well, I'll tell you — my cup pretty much ranneth over at that point. A smile split my face and I felt tears well up in my eyes. At a loss for an appropriate verbal response, I saw no recourse but to make love with Nigel one more time. Nigel didn't fight me on it.

■

"Tell me about Keith." Nigel spoke the sentence into the nape of my neck while his toes toyed with the heel of my right foot.

And I waited for the pain. I felt my spine, my shoulders tense in anticipation of it. And it didn't come. No steel claw closed around my heart; no ball of thorns grew in my throat. Something had changed, lifted, lightened. And for the first time in what may as well have been a hundred years, the taste in my mouth was more sweet than bitter as I spoke his name: "Keith?" I said. "Why Keith?"

"You loved him," Nigel said.

"Damn right," I said, surprised at the feeling of my own lips rising toward a smile. "Keith," I repeated, quietly marveling that it no longer caused me physical pain to say it, wondering what might be appropriate to say about the love of one's life when a cousin who has only recently deposited a copious orgasm across one's chest and belly suddenly says, "Tell me about Keith."

I said, "He had the most beautiful feet."

"Feet?" Nigel said, tickling the sole of my foot with his toes, making me giggle, making me curl up like a shrimp. "You dig feet?"

"Darling," I said, "there is no portion of the male anatomy I do not dig. He called me 'Babe.' Sometimes he called me 'K.T.,' because he thought I looked like the face on Tutankhamen's sarcophagus.

"He sang along, blissfully out of tune, to Bing Crosby records; and would not let me play my David Bowie records when he was in the house. When it got hard, his dick curved just slightly to the right. He cried — I mean tears, streaming — every time he heard me sing 'That Sunday, That Summer.' He kissed better than anybody. Although, I must admit, you have your moments."

"Why, thank you," Nigel said, and gently kissed my neck, my ear.

"He was spoiled," I said. "I mean, I was five or six years getting that man to stop leaving his dirty sweat socks on the bedroom floor. His mother picked up after him all the years he lived at home. And this is a woman who actually vacuumed in high heels and a pearl choker. We're talking a serious Donna Reed fixation here. Whereas Clara's method was to shout something along the lines of—"

Nigel interrupted me: "Boy, you *better* pick up that room of yours, or so help me Hannah, you'll wish you had!"

We clapped hands over our mouths to stifle the laughter. "Athena must have read the same mother manual," I said. We lay together in silence for a minute or two.

"God, I loved that man," I said, not because Nigel wasn't aware of that fact, certainly; but because suddenly I could say it without crying.

"Funny," I said, suddenly daring to talk about it, openly defying the monsters. "We thought we were invincible, simply because we managed to live through the seventies and eighties without getting HIV. We used to talk about what we'd be like as old, old men. White-haired and toothless and still fucking like rabbits. It was like, if AIDS didn't get us, nothing would. Just shows to go ya."

Nigel pulled me tight against his sweat-slick chest. I felt his dick stir and swell into the cleft of my behind. I arched back against it. Not to be outdone, my own cock stretched up and forward, ready to rock and roll, quite oblivious to the weariness of the rest of my body.

"I love you, Captain." He'd whispered it — maybe so that he could have recanted it if it had proved necessary — whispered it so softly that if there had been a mosquito buzzing in the same room, I might have missed it. But I had, indeed, heard. I felt a warmth entirely unrelated to the room temperature spread over me like melting butter, like an angel's idea of Swedish massage, like an anointing of warm oil. My cup ranneth over again. My smile spread with the feeling.

"I told you — I've loved you since I was six years old," Nigel said. Then he added, "I mean it."

"Yes, baby," I said, through the smile, speaking over the strange, arrhythmic one-handed bongo solo that was my heartbeat. "I know you mean it."

Executing a squirming, shoulder-elbow-and-hip turn so that I faced my cousin, I lay practically eyelash-to-eyelash with the achingly beautiful, chocolate-colored, funky-boy-smelling young man who shared some of my blood heritage, some of my taste in pop music, and roughly half a too-small, too-warm bed with me, this man who loved me. I kissed an eyelid, a cheekbone and the dimple just beneath it, one lip and then the other one, and said (louder than a whisper, but not quite aloud), "I love you, too." And by the force with which my cousin's mouth encountered my own, I knew immediately that the bed would get wetter long before it got dryer.

■

"I should go," I said. My lips were heavy with weariness and half-flattened against Nigel's rib cage, and I may or may not have spoken recognizable English. I had no idea what time it was and very little of me actually gave a damn.

"What for?" Nigel said, scratching at the back of my head, his lips barely opening to allow the words to leak out.

"What if somebody came in?" I said.

"It's the middle of the night," Nigel said slowly, as if he were explaining to a small child, or as if he were slip-sliding into sleep.

"In the morning, I mean."

"Don't nobody come in this room," Nigel said.

"I should go," I repeated, though I made no actual move off of Nigel or out of his bed.

"Okay," Nigel said through a yawn that expanded his chest underneath me.

"Okay," I parroted.

"Okay."

■

"What's that you're humming?" Nigel lay against me now, moist back to sticky-wet front, my arm around his waist.

"Hm?"

"You were humming," Nigel said. "A song. What was it?"

"I don't know," I said. My brain was dulled with weariness, my lips only slightly sleepier than my mind. I hadn't fully realized I'd been humming anything at all. And when it came to me, rather than answering Nigel's question, I sang softly to the nape of my cousin's neck: "There was a boy..."

I sang the song one time through, eyes closed, without the smallest shift in my bodily position, in a whisper so intimate an eavesdropper in the hallway with his ear to the door might have thought two large mosquitoes were quarreling over some choice spot to bite.

"'Nature Boy,'" I said and yawned high and wide, and nuzzled the back of Nigel's shorn head.

"Captain," Nigel said, wriggling around to face me.

"What?" I opened one eye to see Nigel's smiling face, his teeth luminous in the semidark.

"You sang," he said.

And I said, "I did?" I kissed the tip of my cousin's nose and said, "Good." And yawned again.

And I thought, I should probably go now.

13.

"Oh, sweet Jesus!"

My eyes popped open to find Athena standing in the doorway in what was probably one of her mother's old faded floral-print housecoats, the morning sun less than flattering on her face. Her eyes were open painfully wide, showing unnatural expanses of white. Her mouth was twisted open along a rough diagonal, exposing the abrupt change of color and evenness where her dental work left off and her remaining natural teeth began. She looked rather as if she had walked in to find Beelzebub, horned and cloven-hoofed, wearing her best dress and taking a large, tar-colored dump in the middle of her kitchen floor.

Her expression told me all I needed to know of her feelings upon finding me in bed with her only son, who, amazingly, was still asleep, and whose right arm was still resting carelessly across my waist. Her exclamation hinted that she was no longer a practicing Muslim.

"Lord Jesus!" Athena cried.

I sat up in bed, clutching the upper sheet to my lap in an uncharacteristic spasm of modesty. Behind me, Nigel stirred. I heard him mumble, "Shot who?" through sleep-heavy lips and then, a good deal louder, "Oh, shit."

"Oh, my Lord Jesus," Athena said, no longer shouting for the moment, her head moving from side to side in a repeated negative.

"Theenie," I began, but then no words came to me. I meant to apologize to her, of course, but the fact was I wasn't sorry I'd slept with Nigel — far from it. I was sorry I hadn't crawled off of my cousin and out of his bed one of the several times I'd said I should, sorry his mother had caught me tucked into the curve of his body come morning, certainly sorry, if not exactly surprised, that the discovery left her upset enough to elicit repeated references to the Master.

"Athena, I—" But still nothing. I glanced back at Nigel, hoping for heaven knows what. The boy sat up in bed, an equivocal little smile skipping about his lips. I looked back to Athena, who sucked in a breath big enough to briefly lend her the appearance of having a bust and used most of it to say, "Your daddy's dead."

And then there was just Athena's faded floral back and the door closing very firmly behind her.

"Shit," I said and then felt a little laugh bubble up from my belly, something between amusement and hysteria. "Shit, shit, shit." I felt Nigel's hand on my shoulder, felt myself lean toward his touch.

"Oh, Johnnie," he said softly, encircling me in his arms, "I'm so sorry."

I stroked his forearms with both hands. "Oh, she'll be all right," I said. "In time. I hope. Besides," I added, "you have to live here with her. I don't."

Nigel dropped his arms from around me and rapped on my head with his knuckles as if knocking on someone's door. "Hello?" he said. "You in there, Cap?"

"What?" I said. Nigel crawled around to face me, one dark, thick eyebrow climbing up nearly to his hairline.

"Captain," he said, touching my face lightly with his fingertips, looking at me as if he half feared his cousin had slipped and fallen off the tightrope of reality and missed the net, as if he half expected me to explode like a homemade bomb. "Didn't you hear? Your father passed."

"Oh," I said. Which is just about all the impact the news seemed to have on me. "Oh."

Funny. I had heard Athena's exit line, loud and clear as a cap pistol going off in the same room. Yet the announcement that my father had died sometime between the previous late afternoon and whatever time of the morning it now was had not affected me in the least. It hadn't even grazed me. Hadn't even managed to push aside my concern over being caught *in flagrante*, or damned close to it, like some philandering husband in a French farce, and stupidly upsetting Athena. And even as I allowed myself to face the fact of my father's death head-on, I quickly realized that the indescribable heart-shredding pain associated with the loss of a loved one (and I'd been there, babe — I'd lived there) had not arrived on the heels of Athena's news flash. And like a dinner guest more than an hour late (no show, no phone call), it seemed likely that it would not arrive at all.

"Cap," Nigel said, his hand falling to my shoulder, "you all right?"

I paused a moment, allowing the pain a chance to come on if it was coming, then nodded. "Yeah," I had to admit. "I'm fine."

"You're fine?" Nigel said. I was pretty sure I knew what he was thinking. That I was numb. That in an automatic spasm of self-preservation, my subconscious was blocking out a twenty-ton Mack truck full of pain, lest my mind should snap like an old guitar string, leaving me to spend the next Lord-knows-how-long staring glassy-eyed through a Librium haze at soap operas in some ill-managed, state-subsidized booby hatch.

"Yes," I said, hoping to convince. I took my cousin's hand in mine and added, "It doesn't hurt a bit. I swear."

Nigel's expression shifted, his nose wrinkled as if I'd farted loudly and long. Instead of fearing for my sanity, he seemed to be wondering what sort of heartless monster might be sitting, cross-legged and quite naked, at the disheveled head of his single bed.

"It's like," I began, not at all sure I could make Nigel understand, not entirely sure I understood myself, "it's like hearing that some stranger died last night. Like reading the obits in the paper and discovering, to my relief, that nobody I know personally is listed. Vaguely sorry that all those strangers died, but only vaguely. You know?"

Nigel shook his head quickly. He didn't know.

I took a deep breath and tried again. "When your grandmother called and told me my father wanted to see me, I hightailed it here as fast as my little legs and Delta Air Lines could carry me. I came here because my father was dying, and despite all the hurt he's caused me over the years, I loved my father. At least, I thought I did." I shrugged. "Now I'm not so sure."

Nigel opened his mouth as if he might speak, but I didn't give him the chance.

"I know I loved him once. I couldn't say when I stopped loving him. Maybe he killed off the last surviving dregs of my love the other day, when he asked for David and ordered me out of his hospital room. Maybe it was when he ordered me and my first boyfriend out of his house. Maybe it was the last time he called me Trixie. I don't know. But now I think I didn't so much love Lance as I really wanted him to love me — which is related, but not really the same thing."

"Captain," Nigel said, "that don't make no kinda sense."

"Oh, it does if you know me," I said. "I have this truly neurotic need to be liked. By everybody. I mean, if the bag boy at the supermarket doesn't smile at me, it can ruin my whole day. If my boss is in a bad mood, it just destroys me. It's one of the many things I'm working through in therapy."

"We're talking about your father," Nigel said, leaning over and applying gentle pressure to my knee with the palm of his hand.

I executed a large, eye-rolling gesture that barely began to express my frustration. "Nigel," I said, topping his hand with my own. "Darling, you never knew your father. And no doubt, you have over the course of your young life concocted a certain number of romantic ideas about what a father is, what having a father means. You may have even come to believe your life would have been better if you'd had a father around, and you may be right. We'll never know."

Shrug.

"I, however, knew my father. And my father was a schmuck."

Nigel cocked his head and looked at me. "Smuck?"

"Schmuck," I repeated, feeling the word with my lips, tasting it on my tongue, relishing the sibilance, the nasal stop, the dull, short vowel, the percussive finish, the near-onomatopoeia of the word as it left my mouth. "I grew up in South Central Los Angeles in the early to mid-sixties, near the intersection of Encroaching Negroes and Rapidly Retreating Jews. So I have always been around a certain number of Jewish people. Also, I was in show business and in show business, *everybody* is Jewish."

"Captain," Nigel said, squeezing my knee again, no doubt concerned that I was rambling, which of course I was. But I would not be deterred.

"Nigel," I said, "American culture has many things for which to thank the Hebrew people. Among them, the Old Testament of the Bible, stand-up comedy, chocolate marble halva, and the word 'schmuck.' My father," I repeated, "was a schmuck. Just the sort of five-star, A-1, lowdown shitheel who could completely write off his first — well, his son, just because that son is gay. Not worth the water expended in crying for him. A schmuck. Pure and simple." My cousin looked at me rather blankly. There was no telling what he might be thinking. "Do you understand what I'm trying to say?" I asked.

"I think so," Nigel said. After a brief pause, he asked, "What's chocolate marble halva?"

I had to smile. "We'll talk about it later," I said. I leaned in and kissed Nigel's lips. "I love you," I said. It's hard to say which felt better. The kiss. Or the saying I love you. Right out loud, Joni, right out loud.

14. One never knows, does one?

So goes one of my favorite Billie Holiday records, "One Never Knows," by Billie Holiday and Her Orchestra, released in 1937 on the Vocalion label. (And a very smart-looking label it is, cobalt blue with gold Gothic-style lettering — I have the 78. Sure, it sounds much better on CD, but there's still something about that label.) The record features Teddy Wilson on piano and Cozy Cole on drums, but not — and I don't know why this is — Lester "Prez" Young (he of the divine fills and solos and the interesting habit of calling everyone "Lady," hence "Lady Day") on tenor sax. Maybe Prez was out of town that day. Maybe he had a sweeter gig, though I can hardly imagine a better way to make a buck than backing Billie Holiday. At any rate, Ben Webster blows tenor here — considerably better than adequate, but no Lester. The record also features a simple but nonetheless legitimate message: You never know when love may come along.

One never knows, does one?

Alice Faye introduced the song in 1936, leaning against a pillar on a cruise ship in the movie *Stow-*

away, starring Shirley Temple and Robert Young. And Alice did a fine job of it, of course, as she nearly always did, enveloping the melody in her inimitable throbbing bass-baritone, carefully enunciating the lyric with her thick, tremulous, shimmeringly glossed lips. But as far as I'm concerned, once Billie wraps that honey-and-sandpaper voice around a song, it's hers, all due respect to Alice.

And there's something about the way Billie drawls and bends her way through the lyric, her sustained notes falling at the ends like a silk scarf tossed through the air, that makes me feel that Lady may well have known firsthand the startling, goosed-from-behind un-predictability of love. That perhaps at some point in her life (perhaps more than one point), she may have allowed herself to do something nearly as ridiculous, nearly as fraught with emotional potholes as, say, falling in love with a close relative little more than half one's age.

And yes, it seemed I was in love with my cousin Nigel. Head-over-butthole. But what could I do, even if I'd wanted to extinguish this sudden and oh-so-welcome resurgence of emotion that had me — the nightmare-haunted, Xanax-popping, not-yet-ready-for-purple widow — feeling better, saner, more blood-pounding alive than I'd felt in far too long?

As Billie also sang: Comes love, nothing can be done.

And as Fats Waller liked to say,

"One never knows, *do* one?"

15. I found Aunt Lucille in the living room, sitting low in her big old armchair. She was wrapped in one of those caftans of hers (this one appropriately black), bare feet flat on the floor, a white cloth tied around her head, not quite concealing the pink plastic-and-foam-rubber curlers in her hair. She seemed to be watching television, only the television wasn't on.

I called her name softly. She looked up and without a word, raised her arms toward me — a gesture so theatrical it reminded me of me. I approached her chair and bent down, and she engulfed me in a rather awkward hug, my face mashed against one of her large, fragrant breasts. She held me for a long moment, rocking softly from side to side, a little atonal hum escaping her throat. It was only after she released me that Lucille finally spoke.

"You poor child," she said. "Your daddy's gone."

I sat back on my heels and looked up into my aunt's face, which seemed somehow blank. Not only did it seem nearly devoid of expression, but her features themselves seemed somehow muted. "Yes, ma'am," I said. "I know."

"My baby brother," she said. I nodded, as it occurred to me what was different about my aunt's face: she hadn't put any makeup on. It had never occurred to me before that she even wore makeup — that my favorite aunt's eyelashes weren't naturally long and curled, her rounded cheeks not possessed of a congenital deep plum-colored blush. A strange sort of blind spot to have about a woman whose name was hardly synonymous with natural beauty — a woman who (to my knowledge) had never worn her naturally kinky hair natural, and whose main source of income was the chemical straightening and curling of the naturally kinky hair shafts of other African-American women. And — I realized even then — this was a very strange sort of thing to notice about a woman in immediate mourning while kneeling before her as if I were some sort of religious pilgrim and the legs of her easy chair were made from pieces of the True Cross. I reached up to touch my aunt's uncharacteristically unadorned cheek and Lucille leaned into my touch, like a big old housecat around suppertime, eyes closed, a little smile on her face. "I'm glad you're here, Junie," she said. I mumbled something inane. True, I was finally glad I'd made the journey to the birthplace, and dying place, of my father — but for reasons having nothing to do either with my father's birth or his recent demise.

"Where's Athena?" I asked, not yet ready to face my cousin, yet all too aware that it must eventually be done.

"She's gone out back," Lucille said. "Mopping the floor in the shop. That's what Theenie does when she's real upset — she cleans. Poor thing," she said. "I never knew she felt so close to her uncle L.J." My aunt took a long, trembling breath. "We'll bury him tomorrow," she said.

"So soon?" I asked.

She nodded her cloth-bound head and shrugged her shoulders at the same time. "No reason to wait," she said. "L.J. made all the arrangements, soon as he got here. Paid for the funeral. Picked out the clothes he wanted to be buried in, right down to the drawers. Ain't but a handful of people left to go the funeral. Your uncle A.J. dead all these twenty-some years, Ruth gone." She closed her eyes and shook her head slowly. "Lord ha' mercy," she said. Then she opened her eyes and addressed me. "Only two things I need for you to do," she said.

"Ma'am?" I had all but made up my mind to pack my bags and get myself ferried out of town on the first available plane.

"I need for you to go down to the funeral parlor today and make sure they made your daddy look all right. Old Fletcher don't always do right. Made A.J. look like some old dead frog." I fought back a smile. I'd attended Uncle A.J.'s funeral. He'd died in his sleep of a heart attack during my junior year in high school, the Rousseau heart being a notoriously defective piece of equipment — I have a murmur, myself. And I vividly remembered him looking very much like an old dead frog.

"And," my aunt said, tapping me softly beneath the chin with her fingertips, "I want you to sing at the funeral."

"Ma'am," I said, "I haven't sung a note in a solid year." I hoped to make it sound as if I was terribly out of practice and leave it at that.

"Then this'll be the first time in a solid year," Lucille said, then smiled a smile that said case closed, done deal.

"You're not about to take no for an answer, are you?"

My aunt shook her head and said, "Mm-mm."

I grasped a chair arm and pulled myself to my feet, my leg muscles having begun an 1812 Overture of pain.

I sat back into the smaller, considerably less comfortable chair parked at a right angle to Lucille's and stretched my knotted legs. "You want me to sing at the funeral, even knowing how I feel about him?" I asked.

"You won't be singin' for him," she said. "You'll be singin' for me." My aunt smiled a wide, warm smile that suddenly made her look as if she were wearing makeup. "I love to hear you sing."

"Really?" I felt a smile pulling at my face.

"Since you was just a little bitta boy," she said. "You prob'ly won't remember, but I recall one time, you must not a' been more than five or six years old." She tilted her head to one side and smiled, seemingly enjoying the mind movie of the memory, or perhaps the act of remembering itself. "We were all sitting in the back room there: your mama, your daddy — your uncle Chester was still alive then. Your little brother was just out of diapers, seems like." I watched my aunt's eyes glisten with new tears, watched her blink them back. "Lord ha' mercy," she said. "Must be thirty years." She closed her eyes, took in a long breath, let it out. "You were sittin' over against the wall, next to that big old Philco stand-up radio we used to have back there. The radio was on, playing some song. Just some bop-a-dop song — Athena must have had it on, she was just calling herself some kinda teenager at that time."

Then Lucille looked directly into my face and said, "And you was singing, singing along with the radio. And there was something about your voice that, that made me want to cry. It wasn't just that it was so pretty, so high and so sweet. It was—" She looked away from me, her right hand fluttering along her bosom. "There was this, this little sadness in your voice. A little—" She clenched her fist against her deep chest and crunched her face into itself as if recoiling from a stabbing pain. "It was as if you had known heartache," she said, "like your little heart had been broken. And you wasn't but five or six years old, you see. And I turned to your mama and I said, 'Clara, that child has got himself a voice, honey.'"

I sat up straighter in my chair as my head lit up with the memory. "I remember that," I said. "But for some reason, I remember it being Aunt Ruth."

Lucille shook her head. "No, baby. Was me. And every since that time, anytime I heard you singing, I was listening for that little heartbreak in your voice. Your mama's got it too, you know."

"Yes, I know. What would you like me to sing?"

"'Steal Away,'" she said, without hesitation. "'Steal Away to Jesus.'"

"Was it Dad's favorite spiritual?"

She shook her head. "Mine," she said. "You know it?"

I smiled.

There are songs — I've never stopped to count them, but they are legion — songs that I've known for so long, I don't remember ever not knowing them, don't remember ever consciously learning them. It seems they have always been part of me. This comes from being raised by Clara Jane Rousseau, a woman who (for at least as long as I have been alive and sentient) has always sung the way most people take in oxygen and breathe out CO_2, effortlessly, without conscious thought. It comes from growing up in the Church of God in Christ and the black Baptist church, churches where music seemed to make up three-quarters of services that began around eleven on Sunday morning and made a kid feel lucky if he was out the door and into the sunshine by two; churches where the minister or some fan-wielding brother or sister in the congregation might take a song away from the choir and make it his own, executing an impromptu solo or obligato for a chorus or two, and where the sermon itself might be at least half sung. It comes from having attended elementary schools where casual groups of black fifth-graders leaning against the playground fence could sing better than many white high school choirs. This body of music has been so much a part of me for so long that it has at times seemed that there was no air that I breathed that did not contain that music, those songs.

Spirituals, mostly: "Joshua Fit the Battle of Jericho," "Elijah Rock." "Were You There When They Crucified My Lord." "Steal Away" was very much a part of my life repertoire.

So when Lucille asked me if I knew "Steal Away to Jesus," I could say without hesitation, "Yes. I know it."

"I knew you did," she said. "Thank you. And, baby —" She raised a forefinger. "Your daddy could be a asshole, excuse my French. But I do believe he loved his children." She opened her palm as if to forestall my protest — not that I had plans to raise one. "And I believe that way deep down, you love him, too."

I didn't respond. Lucille did not ask me to. What did it matter now, anyway?

As I began to push myself up from the chair, my aunt stopped me with an upraised forefinger. "Junie," she said, and I fell back into a seated position. "I know you think I don't know what you've been through this past year. I know you think don't nobody know the trouble you seen. But let me tell you something." She tapped on her deep bosom with her gesturing finger. "Quiet as it's kept," she said, "I'm almost sixty-seven years old." Looking at my aunt's face, quite unlined even sans makeup, it was hard to believe. She shook her head, as if she could barely believe it herself.

"Almost twice your age," she continued. "You say good morning and good evening as many times as I have, you — well, you get old, for one thing. And," she raised that finger again, "you learn. I've buried me two husbands. Lost another one to a blackjack dealer with silicones in her chest." She snorted a little laugh through her nose. "I learned from that, too. Lemme tell you one of the things I've learned over this life of mine."

She leaned forward a little in her chair. "Everybody wants to be happy, but not a whole lots of people ever is. Most people is happy at least some of the time. Notice those times. Enjoy those times. Save those times, make a little box in your heart to keep 'em in, so you can take 'em out, hold 'em in your hands, and look 'em over sometimes when you ain't so happy. Thank God for those times."

Lucille leaned forward farther, and touched my knee with the fingertips of one hand. She looked me full in the face, and as I looked back at my aunt, she looked to me to be far younger than her nearly sixty-seven years, and at the same time looked every minute of it.

"'Cause sometimes, Junie — maybe for weeks, maybe for months at a time, maybe even for most of your life — the best you can hope for is to wake up in the morning, alive and in your right mind. Just breathing and not crazy." She leaned back into her chair and said, "And you should fall to your knees and say, 'Thank you, Jesus,' for that."

"And what about those times when all you can be sure of is the breathing part?"

Lucille raised her eyes toward heaven — a place I had no doubt she believed existed, big and literal, eighteen-karat sidewalks, starry crowns, a pair of big white wings and everything, some great Boca Raton in the sky where she expected to retire for eternity — and said, "You just got to leave it in the hands of the Lord."

I thought she might say something like that.

"Thank you, ma'am," I said, rising from my chair. "I think I'll go see Athena." She had to be dealt with, sooner or later, and this seemed as good a time as any.

As I leaned over and kissed my aunt's smooth cheek, the telephone rang, long and jangling. Lucille's telephones were both big, old black dial phones, with bells like fire engines.

In one of those strange, rather frightening flashes of clairvoyance which strike me only rarely (Thank Heaven!) and absolutely never when I could really use one, I knew immediately who was calling. I mean, knew for sure. I straightened up quickly and beating my aunt to the punch, I picked up the receiver in the middle of the second ring.

"Mom?"

"Hello, baby," came my mother's soft midalto voice, the sound coming in a bit scratchy, like an old record album. She didn't bother to mention the fact that I had known it was she on the phone, all the way from Paris, any more than I'd bother asking how she had known where to find me — in my haste, I'd neglected to call and tell her I was going anywhere. After all, this was the woman who had dreamed Nigel's birth on the very night he was born, complete with a talking stork who informed her of the exact time of the birth and the baby's weight, to the ounce. She had also received a clear premonition of her own mother's death, mere minutes before my grandmother succumbed to a heart attack. And while my own psychic spasms were few and far between, Mom knew this peculiar blessing-and-curse was as much a part of her legacy to me as my cheekbones and my singing voice. "Your daddy's dead," she said. It wasn't a question.

I said, "Yes."

From her chair, Lucille pointed to the telephone and whispered, "Your mama?" I nodded yes, and Lucille returned the nod, obviously no more surprised than I at my mother's call.

"I had a little vision," my mother said, the way some women might say she had a little allergy attack. "Your grandmother Eudora came and told me." After a static-filled moment, Mom said, "How you doing?"

I considered the question for a bit, then said, "Breathing and not crazy."

"Well, thank the good Lord for that," she said. I rather thought she might. There followed a few moments of transatlantic dead air. I filled a bit of it by saying, "He loved you. He told me so."

"Well," she said, "he always did have the funniest ways of showing his love."

I had to smile. "Well," I said, "at least he said he loved you. That's more than he managed to say about me before kicking the proverbial bucket."

"Schmuck!" I heard my mother say.

"What?"

"Daniel taught me that word," she said. "Schmuck. Your daddy was a schmuck."

"Mom!" I wasn't so much shocked that she'd speak of my late father in such a manner as I was surprised she was familiar with the word "schmuck."

"I'm sorry, baby," she said quickly, "I know I shouldn't be speaking ill of the dead. I didn't want to talk about him, no-way. I just wanted to see how you were holding up."

"Still standing," I said. "But the day is young."

"You know I'm praying for you," she said, and I heard her voice crumple as she attempted to add, "Always." Even long-distance, I could tell she was crying.

"Mom? You all right?"

I heard a wet sniff, a couple of quick, hiccupping breaths.

Another sniff, and then I heard her swear under her breath — or her quaint version of swearing: "Got-dog-git," she said. And then, "Yeah, baby. I'm okay. Let me yell at Lucille for a minute."

"Sure," I said, and then, "Hello to Daniel for me."

"We leaving next week," she said. "I'll call you when we get back." She took a breath, then added, "I love you, baby."

"I love you, too." I held the phone out toward my aunt. "Clara?" she said, taking the receiver to her ear. "How you doin', cher?"

I did a little bye-bye wave in my aunt's direction and started again toward the back door, nearly colliding with Nigel at the kitchen doorway.

"You gonna go try and talk to Muh?" he said, just above a whisper, resting the fingers of one hand against my chest.

"Yeah." I found myself, without thinking, leaning toward my cousin.

"You want me to go with you?"

I shook my head no. "You can deal with whatever's between you and your mom later," I said. "I've got to deal with what's between her and me."

"She must be real pissed," Nigel said. "I can hear her mopping from here."

"Nigel," Lucille called from the next room, "baby, come see."

"Yes, ma'am," Nigel said.

I kissed my cousin's lips, barely grazed them, really, and said, "Wish me luck."

■

Athena was still mopping as I opened the door of the beauty shop, wiped my feet several times on the ancient rubber doormat, and took one slow, careful step inside. Her body swung up and down from the waist, her elbows pumped vigorously up and down, the muscles stood out in her slender arms as she worked. She emitted a little grunt with each down-and-forward stroke of the old-fashioned string-head mop she applied to the floor as if trying to wipe her mind clean of the image of her male cousin and her only son lying moist and naked, side by side in a rumpled single bed.

Standing in the doorway on as little of the wet floor as possible, I called her name. She grunted a bit louder on the next stroke, but otherwise did not acknowledge my existence. "Athena," I said a bit louder, "are we going to talk about this?"

"Hell, no," she said, her gaze still focused on the floor beneath her.

"Athena," I said, stepping forward, "would you give the kid a break, already?"

She stopped in midmop and leaned hard against the handle. She spoke through clenched teeth and curled lips: "I'd like to break your god-damn neck. Now, get your god-damn dirty feet off my god-damn clean floor and get out of here!"

"Dammit, Athena." I took a few more steps toward her, holding on to stationary objects — a big, old dryer chair, the counter — against the near inevitability of slipping on the wet floor and breaking every bone in my face. "I never meant to hurt you. You know I didn't."

"Well then, I don't know what you call yourself meanin' to do," she said, applying a fist to one blue-jeaned hip, "comin' into my house and—" She made a sour face and a wavy hand gesture. "With my boy." Her formerly Muslim, currently very angry mind could obviously find no words for what she imagined had gone on between Nigel and myself.

"Theenie," I said, steadying my footing against the counter, "I was hurting. I needed somebody. And Nigel was there. If you're waiting for me to say I'm sorry he was there, well, I'm not sorry. I'm sorry you walked in on us, and I'm sorry you're upset, but that's it. And let me be the first to clue you in: your 'boy' is fully grown, and queer."

I heard the crack of Athena's hard, wet palm against my face a split second before I felt the sting, a zillion miniature needles in the shape of a hand. "He's not!" she said, a look on her face just a scream away from the funny farm.

"Shit-damn, Athena!" I touched the side of my face gingerly with my fingertips and listened to my ears ring for a moment. I could feel my skin beginning to swell. Within a few minutes, my cousin's handprint would stand out clearly in a rosy bas-relief. I have very sensitive skin — always have. "Feel better now?" I said.

"Some," said Athena. "Feel a whole lot better once you're out of my house, away from my son. I swear, I used to think you had some decency."

"Theen—," I started, but then thought, What the hell? How could I explain? I couldn't make her understand how I felt about Nigel — not soon, maybe not ever, certainly not right then, standing flat-footed on wet linoleum with a prickling handprint on my face and blood lust in Athena's eyes. "Forget it," I said, turning rather clumsily, as if on roller skates for the first time. "I'm out of here."

"Damn right you're out of here," Athena said. "I want you out of my house — today."

"What?" I turned back a little too quickly and just caught my balance against one of the two big swiveling chairs bolted to the floor.

"You heard me," she said with a little head toss. "Get out."

I looked at my cousin, leaning against her mop handle, hand to hip, chin jutting forward: a second-rate actress playing to the cheap seats. A lifelong drama queen myself, I knew a great big footlights-and-grease-paint *scene* when I saw one.

I decided to call her bluff. I smiled and said, "All right. I believe I'll go and say good-bye to Aunt Lucille now, if you don't mind," and started for the door.

"What?" Athena said, her voice sliding up an octave over the length of the word. I was right: she no more wanted this particular cup of tea spilled into her mother's lap than she wanted to grow a handlebar mustache.

"I said, I'm going to let your mother know I've no place to sleep the night before my father's funeral, and I'm going to tell her why." I was down the stairs and into the backyard when I heard Athena screech my name. There was a thump and crash from behind me and I heard Athena yell, "Shit," and then call my name again.

"Junie!" she screamed yet again, shoving the screen door so hard it slapped against the wall and running buh-buh-buh-bump down the wooden stairs.

Aunt Lucille was standing in the back doorway when I reached it, Athena barely two steps behind me, her breathing clearly audible.

Lucille punched both fists into her ample hips and said, "What the ham-fat is going on back here?" Aunt Lucille's adorable surrogate for "What the hell." (Another one of my favorites is her substitute for "Got-dammit": "Got no sense a-tall!")

"Well," I said, the picture of David Niven-ish composure, "it seems Athena has ordered me from her house."

"Athena," Aunt Lucille said, turning to her daughter, "you got a house?" Then back to me, "Now, Junie, why would your cousin send you out of this house?"

"Would you like to tell her," I said to Athena, "or shall I?"

"Junie!" Athena said, her jaw clenched.

"Nigel already told me," Lucille said, with the smug look of someone getting the last laugh.

"What?" Athena and I exclaimed in stereo.

"That's right," Lucille said. "Now you two big babies get in this house right now." She held the door open wide. I made an expansive gesture of allowing Athena in first. She shot me a gonad-withering glance.

"Why don't we all sit down," Lucille said. Nigel was already seated at the kitchen table eating a bowl of Cheerios, making a big point out of reading the back of the box. Lucille took a seat, folding her hands on the table in front of her. Athena, visibly atremble (likely with rage, I thought), sat opposite her. As I took the chair across from Nigel, our eyes met and I watched a little smile skitter across his face. He'd probably been looking forward to a confrontation not unlike this one for quite some time. His smile dropped quickly and he said, "What happened to your face?"

"I fell down," I said, deadpan, still feeling the sting of Athena's palm, imagining the raised handprint on my face.

"Muh," Nigel turned to Athena, "you hit the Captain?"

"Shut up," Athena said, her lips barely moving.

"You hit him!" Nigel said.

"Ahma be hittin' all over your black ass in a minute," Athena said, her lips curling over her dental work. "What you mean startin' this mess with your cousin in my house?"

"Ain't none of your house, no-way," Nigel countered. "It's Queenie's house."

"Now y'all just listen here," Lucille said, slapping her palm against the tabletop, making a sound similar enough to a gunshot to startle both Nigel and Athena into silence. "I don't pretend to understand what's been going on between Nigel and Junie. Now, I know about gay." She paused a moment for effect. "Y'all didn't invent that. But I can't say I understand about two young men cousins. I just don't know. I ain't sayin' I think it's right and I ain't in no position to judge and tell you it's wrong. That's between y'all and the Lord," she said, looking first at me and then at Nigel.

"Muh—," Athena attempted to interrupt, but Lucille cut her off with, "Girl, shut up." She cleared her throat and continued. "Now, my last brother done died this morning. And I got to tell you, I don't feel quite right sitting here at my kitchen table talking about sex — homo or regular or no kind — with my baby brother not hardly cold yet. But I'll say this: I won't have no not-married folks sleeping together in my house." She looked Athena dead in the eye and repeated, "My house. I didn't allow it with you," she said, indicating her daughter with a nod of the head, "and I ain't allowing it with you." She inclined her head toward Nigel. "Now as for you," she said, pointing an index finger in my direction, "I already told you I want you here to help me with the funeral. But I want you to promise me that you and this one ain't gonna be messin' around in here when I already told you I won't have it."

"Actually," I said, "I think I should just go."

"Go?" said Aunt Lucille. "What you mean, go?"

"Find someplace else to stay the night." I could see Lucille's face preparing for protest, but I didn't give her the chance. "Look," I said, speaking directly to my aunt, "Athena has made it clear to me that my presence here makes her uncomfortable. And, frankly, I can under-stand that. This may not be her house," I said, "but it is her home." Suddenly very aware of my rudeness in speaking of my cousin as if she were either absent or less than sentient, I turned to Athena and said, "Your home." And to Lucille: "I think I know a place I can stay for a night or two. I'm sure I won't be here any longer than that."

"Where?" Aunt Lucille asked.

"Anna Lee's," I said.

"You know you don't have to do that," Lucille said.

"I think it's best," I said, looking first at my aunt, and then at her daughter, whose eyes shot death rays into me from across the table.

"Well, if the Captain's going," Nigel said, "I'm going, too."

"Oh, no, you ain't," Athena said, punctuating each word with a head wag. Nigel rolled his eyes toward the ceiling. "And don't you be rolling them big eyes at me," Athena said. "I'll slap the black off you."

"Yeah, right," Nigel said, rising from the table. To me, he said, "I'll run you over to the funeral home whenever you're ready." And he left the room without another word.

Leaving me with the women. Athena's anger was a palpable force in the room, like the heat outdoors. I made another feeble attempt to apologize. "I said it before and I meant it," I said to the clenched fist that was Athena's face. "I never meant for you to get hurt." Athena stood so quickly and with such force that the chair overturned and crashed to the floor. Acknowledging neither the toppled furniture nor me, she left the room, heading toward her bedroom.

"Well," I said after a moment.

"You still don't have to go," Lucille said.

"Yes," I said. "I do. But thank you. For being so understanding about — everything."

"Now, I don't want you getting the idea I *approve* of what's been going on here. 'Cause I don't. But you're fully grown. And much as Athena don't want to admit it, so is Nigel. Ain't my job to disapprove. Ain't my place."

"Well," I said, desperate for an exit line, "thanks anyway." And rose from the table.

16.

Waxy.

It was the first word that came to my mind upon viewing the newly embalmed remains of my father. Not just the word, of course, but like just about everything else I ever think or say, it was a line from something: in this case, *Greater Tuna*, the play, which Keith and I had seen in San Francisco six, seven years before. A company of two (count 'em, two) actors (a big, rotund, dark one and a small, compact, sandy blond one) portrayed the entire population of Tuna, a tiny, fictional town in Texas — men, women, kids, pets. At one point, two of the female inhabitants of the town are standing in the funeral parlor over somebody's open casket, criticizing the local undertaker's technique. The smaller one, Vera Carp, peers down through her cat's-eye glasses, runs her fingertip along the cheek of the corpse, rubs the finger against her thumb, and says (in this tight little Texas accent), "Waxy."

Why does my mind do these things to me?

Indeed, my father's face did look rather as if his cheeks had been smeared with rouge by someone with absolutely no sense of the tasteful use of makeup, then painted with paraffin. The culprit was a Mr. Fletcher Beaufait, the proprietor and chief technician of the Beaufait Funeral Home. Mr. Beaufait was a tall, light-skinned gentleman with old-style processed (probably dyed) black hair, a pencil-line mustache, and a bodily scent composed of equal parts formaldehyde and entirely too much Brut cologne. He had taken my right hand in both of his and mouthed some platitudes I couldn't manage to make myself hear, before leading me and Nigel into the tiny broom closet of a room containing a bouquet of dusty plastic flowers on an easel, and my father in an obviously inexpensive coffin.

I looked into the casket and fought the urge to touch the waxed cheek of the artificial-looking face that only vaguely resembled my mental picture of my father.

"Funny," I said to Nigel, who stood to my right side and just a half step behind me. "As many funerals, memorial services, and wakes as I've attended over the past few years, I've really never seen very many dead people." Nigel made no reply, not that I required one. "Keith, of course," I continued, realizing even as I a spoke that I was rambling, but unable to stop myself. "And Crockett Miller — I gave the eulogy at his service. But for the most part, the people I've lost were either so frightfully wasted away that it would have been cruel to all concerned to have an open casket. Or else the relatives came swooping down and carried them away to Pocatello or Sheboygan or wherever they came from."

I looked down at the stuffed and mounted remains of the man whose bodily fluids caused me to be. By the sweat of whose brow I ate bread for the first eighteen years of my life and who had been — oh, dear Lord — my first crush, or something frighteningly similar. Is there a Freudian term for that? Did the Greeks have a word for it? I looked at all that was left of the man who had hurt me more than I ever dreamed I could hurt and live to tell the tale. I looked at my father's painted and paraffin-coated carcass and said, "Mr. Beaufait went a little heavy on the eye shadow, don't you think? He made Daddy look rather like an old queen."

Nigel, probably beginning to fear for my sanity (and not entirely without reason, I suppose), reached for my hand and held it in his. I gripped his hand hard as the pain seemed to snap my sternum in two and tears fell warm and stinging from my eyes.

"Damn," I said, phlegm gargling at the back of my throat. "It's just not fuckin' fair!"

"What?" Nigel asked, stroking my arm.

"You can't stop loving them," I blubbered, "no matter what they do to you. No matter how they hurt you. No matter what."

Nigel encircled my shoulders with his long arms and held me, rocking me softly while I trembled and wept. "I know," he said. "It's a fuckin' curse."

And as I stood there next to a particle-board box of my father's overly made-up bodily remains, weeping an irregularly shaped stain onto the shoulder of Nigel's shirt, the idea slowly crept up on me: Perhaps Aunt Lucille had been right. That just as I seemed to have no control over loving my sometimes hateful, more often utterly indifferent father, perhaps — utterly in spite of himself — he had had no choice but to love me, his son. And that, lacking any recent evidence, verbal or otherwise, that this was in fact the case, I was forced either to choose to believe it anyway — to take it on faith, as Clara would say — or simply learn to do without.

It wasn't much, but there it was.

I sniffed a big wet one and, releasing myself from my cousin's arms, retrieved my handkerchief from my pocket and blotted my eyes before honking a huge wad into the cloth.

"Thank you," I said to Nigel. "And in the words of Eddie Jefferson, I'm through."

■

Billie sang, "Comes love, nothing can be done" from the big old Magnavox. I half sat, half reclined on Anna Lee's great hulk of a sofa, a cushion at my back and Nigel against my front, his nearly hairless head just below my chin, the small of his back between my thighs. Even with Nigel's long legs stretched out full-length, there was plenty of room for Anna Lee to sit at the opposite end of the couch, cross-legged and nursing an immense cup of darkly fragrant coffee, humming softly along with Billie.

I had been so debilitated by my visit to the mortuary (small personal revelations notwithstanding, I left the funeral home feeling rather as if I had just completed a triathlon with a small Japanese-made car strapped to my back), I'd crawled into Anna Lee's guest bed and slept a blissfully dreamless sleep for the remainder of the afternoon. Nigel had kissed me awake (a fairy-tale prince in blue jeans) in time for a supper of jambalaya, the likes of which I had never before experienced: rich and fishy, spicy enough to bring tears and to open every sinus and pore, and prepared by my hostess with what seemed equal parts of cayenne pepper, heart, and soul. Now, my head still a bit foggy with sleep, I was seemingly past the sobbing stage (for the time being, at least) and contented to feel the weight of my cousin's body against my own and to strum the ripples of his hard belly with my fingers to the soft beat of Lady's music.

"This is good," I said, referring to the music, the softness of the sofa, the hardness of my cousin, the soft light from the several motley lamps in the room, the residual tang of the jambalaya at the back of my tongue, and the immediate feeling of being alive and clothed in what passes for one's right mind.

"She sure could sing," said Anna Lee.

"If there's a Jazz Heaven," I said, "you know they got one hell of an alto section." Which elicited a giggle from Anna Lee.

After a moment, Nigel said, "You believe in heaven, Cap?"

"Heaven?" I repeated. It wasn't so strange, considering recent events, for the conversation to shift from the musical to the metaphysical. I gave the question a long moment's thought. "No," I said, finally. "I don't suppose I do. Heaven knows—" I rolled my eyes at my own slip of the tongue. "Sometimes I wish I could believe in a better home a-waiting in the sky, as the song says. Always howdy-howdy, and never good-bye. Not so much for myself but, like ... for my mom. And Aunt Lucille and, like — Mahalia Jackson. People who really believe, but really. I'd hate to see them disappointed."

"Maybe there is one for them," Nigel said.

"Could be, Junior," I said. "But not for me, as Ira Gershwin once said. I just don't buy it. Not since I was a kid. Lately, I've grown fond of the notion of reincarnation."

"You buy all that Shirley MacLaine stuff?" Nigel said.

"Well, Shirley didn't exactly invent that stuff," I said, not surprised and yet a tiny bit bothered that Nigel was so quick to pooh-pooh the closest thing to religious beliefs I could currently claim. "And to be perfectly honest, to say I believe in reincarnation — like put-a-gun-against-my-head, absolute belief — would be an exaggeration. It just makes sense to me, you know? Just rational sense." Shrug. "Maybe I just like the idea of having another shot at it. And then another. Like retakes.

"I don't know if I have anything I really, really believe in. I used to tell Keith the only thing I really believed in was him and me." I tapped the crown of Nigel's head with my fingers. "How about you, Skeezix? You believe in heaven?"

Nigel didn't answer right away. "Sometimes I believe," he said. "Maybe it's just because Queenie always said so. Sometimes, I don't know. I mean, if there's heaven, then there's probably hell, too, right? And if God made us all and loves us all, how could He send some people to heaven and some to hell? On the other hand, maybe there should be a hell, just so, like, Hitler and Charles Manson and them can go." He shook his head as if to clear it. "I don't know," he said. "You believe in heaven, Anna Lee?"

She held up a shielding palm, lowered her head, and said, "Sorry, boys. There's not a whole lot of subjects I won't talk about, but religion is definitely one of them."

"All right," I said, "new subject: Anna Lee," I said, doing my best Barbara Walters interview. "What's a top-notch Creole-Cajun cook and connoisseur of fine jazz vocals like yourself doing in a sleepy little backwater like this?"

"This sleepy little backwater is my home," she said toward her coffee cup, then turned to me and added, "I was born not far from this house. I went away to school, but I came back to teach. I belong here."

I feared I had offended my hostess. "I didn't mean anything against this place," I said. "My people were born here, both sides of my family. And up until the previous generation, they all died here, too. I just meant — well, don't you get bored?"

Anna Lee smiled and shook her head slowly. "Oh, no, darlin'," she said. "The folks around here are a lot of things, but they sho' ain't boring. And it's not as if I never get out of this house. I teach. And I have friends among those who choose not to believe that I run a combination opium den and whorehouse in my living room. I even date, on rare occasion. And we're not so far from New Orleans that I can't get there now and then. I keep busy."

"You ever been married?" I asked. I wanted to know something of this odd little coffee-colored woman who'd so closely befriended my Nigel, who tossed the meanest jambalaya I'd ever experienced, and whose love of good pop vocals seemed at least as deep as my own. I'd listen to anything she might choose to tell me.

"Years ago," she said, her face falling just perceptibly. She tapped the rim of her coffee cup with a fingernail. "We loved each other, and then we didn't. Could we change the subject, please?"

"We could go back to religion," Nigel said with one of those bad-boy smiles of his.

Anna Lee crossed her arms over her chest, and suddenly I feared Nigel had made her angry. She said, "You want to know what I believe in? I believe in life." She pointed down toward the floor. "This one. I believe this is it. You get born and then after a few years, you get dead. Period." She smiled a little, and said, "So you best enjoy as much of this life as you can. Be it the man in your arms, or a plate of crawfish etouffe, or 'Struttin' with Some Barbecue' by Louis Armstrong and the Hot Five."

She turned and looked me in the face. "Squeeze that man tight," she said. "Clean your plate. Get up and shake your ass to that music, baby. 'Cause this is all there is. End of sermon." She tilted her chin downward and offered us a sly, upward glance. She smiled a small, knowing smile and said, "Can you dig it?"

I smiled in return, nodded.

"I knew you could," she said.

■

It must have been nearly one in the morning. Nigel, Anna Lee, and I had sat, listening to record after record. The singers were all musicians we called by their first names, as if we were friends — Ella, Billie, Aretha, Pops. We'd talked little, except to exclaim something along the lines of "Lord, that bitch could stone *sing!*" Then, well after midnight, Anna Lee wished us both night-night, sleep tight, don't let the mosquito bite, and padded off to bed. I was more than ready to follow her example, when I noticed a copy of *I'll Buy You a Star* by Johnny Mathis propped up against the cabinet of the stereo set.

It was one of my favorite albums from my childhood, one of the albums Clara played at night as she tucked David and me into bed during the years when we lived in South Central L.A., back when Lance worked some ninety miles away in Victorville and only came home on weekends. It was one of the albums she played so often that I had memorized every note, every breath, every orchestra cue. And one I hadn't been able to locate in any rare-record store or bargain bin I'd searched, and I'd searched hundreds.

And I had to hear it.

Nigel stayed up to listen with me, half lying against me, back-to-front on the sofa (a position I'd quickly learned to love), eyes closed but obviously not sleeping, humming along now and then.

During the first verse of "Stairway to the Stars," Nigel lifted himself from the couch, stood over me with his right hand outstretched, and said, "Dance with me."

"What?"

"Dance," he said.

The music was soft, and played at a low decibel level so as not to disturb Anna Lee. And it was a ballad, rich with strings and pregnant with romance as only a Johnny Mathis ballad can be, so there was no way Nigel was inviting me to get up and shake my groove thing — even if I could remember where I'd left it.

"I only know how to follow," I said, taking Nigel's hand.

"Cool," Nigel said. "I only know how to lead."

I rose, rested my right hand in the palm of Nigel's long-fingered left, placed my left in the general vicinity of Nigel's right shoulder blade, Mathis sang about sailing away on lazy daisy petals, Nigel moved with the music, his movements small and soft as the ballad itself, and I moved with him.

I've never been much good at slow dance. Now, in my day I was known to boogie with the best of them, the potent mix of a thunderous synthesized beat, hypnotically repetitious Donna Summer vocal, and my own youthful abandon grabbing me by the pelvis and shoulders and carrying me a good three-quarters of the way back to the Motherland. But, Great Goshamighty, don't ask me to box-step. It has always required a very good slow dancer with a certain amount of physical strength to lead me around a floor and make me look even passably graceful.

The last man to accomplish this feat had been Keith Keller. Nigel Walker was nearly as good. Leaning close against my cousin's body, I nuzzled the warm, smooth skin of his neck, blissfully unconcerned with my feet.

"You ready to sing tomorrow?" Nigel asked.

"Looking forward to it," I said. Following my father's funeral the next afternoon, I'd be heading back home, a prospect which I faced with decidedly mixed emotions.

"I'm going to miss you so much," I said.

"Don't start missing me yet," he answered. "I'm here now." I held him tighter in lieu of verbal reply. Being in the moment, being "here now" as my yoga instructor used to say, has never been one of my stronger suits. I wanted to say so much to my cousin as we swayed together, Mathis's sweet caress of a voice all around us. I wanted to say "love" over and over and over, repeat the words "I love you," until they ceased to make sense. I wanted to thank him for loving me. For helping me to remember how it felt to love someone and be loved in return. For pointing me back toward Los Angeles a slightly saner, a bit more peaceful, somewhat happier thirty-something-year-old black queer widow-man than when I'd arrived a few days before.

What I did say was, "I've got a chub."

"What?" Nigel said.

"I'm popping a serious boner, here." Which in fact, I was. The same thing used to happen when I slow-danced with Keith.

Nigel removed his left hand from my right and did a pantomime of looking at a watch he was not, in fact, wearing. "My goodness," he said, "just look at the time. We best get to bed."

We headed down the hall toward Anna Lee's guest bedroom, hand in hand, leaving Johnny Mathis to finish "Stairway to the Stars" all by himself.

Wade in the water
Wade in the water, children
Wade in the water
God's gon' trouble
The water.

■

A small group of black folk — seventeen by my quick count, including myself — of both genders and widely varying ages, sat in an old one-room whitewashed Louisiana church house, singing. We sang a song older than the oldest person in the room by a couple of hundred years, at least (and there was a woman not of my acquaintance in a white dress, seated a couple of rows behind me, who looked to be a hundred if she was a day). We sang without the benefit of grand piano or pipe organ or so much as a tambourine, seventeen voices raised in simple harmony, accompanied only by the clapping of hands and the stomping of shod feet on a humidity-dampened, humidity-warped old wooden floor.

See that host all dressed in white

sang the very Lynn-Yvette Mayall I had met in Aunt
Lucille's beauty shop. With her black-pillbox-hatted
head back, eyes closed, right hand furiously working a
paper Beaufait Funeral Home fan in a doomed attempt
to cool her large, floral-print-dressed body, but barely
disturbing the great drops of sweat hanging like bugle
beads from her great, round, ebony face, she sang in a
serrated-edged alto that cut through the moist, heavy
air. We the congregation answered her,

God's gon' trouble the water,

continuing the call-and-response tradition of African-
American vocal music that began in the Motherland,
probably not long after man found his voice, and
schlepped to these shores in fetters with the singers, to
be continued through slavery and into freedom, carried
from the field to the church and back out into the field
again, and finally into recording studios and onto metal
and wax, onto acetate and tape, onto the *Billboard* R&B
charts. I'm talking doo-wop, I'm talking girl groups, I'm
talking the Supremes: for what, after all, is Diana
singing, "Where did our love go," with Mary and Flo
chiming in, "Baby-baby, ooh-baby-baby," if not good
old African-tribal-chant-cum-field-holler call-and-
response, all done up in bouffant wigs and spike-heeled
pumps? Let the church say: Amen.

Look like the children of the Is-rae-lites
God's gon' trouble the water.

And Lord have mercy, didn't it feel good, to sing and
sing out loud, running music through a body far too
long devoid of music, clapping and stomping and doing
the Ray Charles side-to-side rock from the waist. It had
been twenty years at least since I'd seen the inside of a
black church, more than that since I'd been in a
Holiness Church like this one, the Holy Cross Church

of God in Christ, the church where both my mother and my father had been brought up. It was a church whose members were given to spiritual ecstasies that exhibit themselves in shouting, fainting spells, seeming gibberish misdesignated the Gift of Tongues, and the so-called Holy Dance, which for my money always seemed the "Patty-Duke-Show"-look-alike cousin of the decidedly unholy dances of the likes of James Brown and Tina Turner. It was a church where a woman wearing a sleeveless dress, open-toed shoes, or what anyone in the building might decide was an excess of makeup would be turned away at the door. It was a church where the knowledge of my personal sexual proclivities — let alone what I had perpetrated with my cousin Nigel over the past couple of days — might easily prove ample excuse for a Deliverance from Unclean Spirits, a Protestant version of good old-fashioned exorcism. Still, for sheer exuberance and the raw beauty of the human voice raised in song, unaccompanied, you could hardly beat the singing.

Nigel, my cousin and partner-in-crime-against-nature, sat to my right, looking like a little kid dressed up for Sunday school in a wide, gray-striped necktie and a white short-sleeved dress shirt already nearly transparent with his sweat. He was singing and clapping and stomping with the rest if not the best of them — it wasn't as if he couldn't carry a tune in a pickup truck, he just wasn't a singer. His grandmother sat to the left of me in a black dress that fit close to her voluptuous-looking form and a brimless hat with a veil that obscured her face to the mouth. She neither sang nor clapped, but swayed quietly from side to side with the beat of the music, her black-gloved hands folded in her lap, moving to the song she requested be sung at this her baby brother's funeral, a song closely associated with baptism, rather than death. Perhaps Lucille had focused on baptism as symbolic death, burial, and resurrection. Or perhaps my aunt was simply being contrary. Or maybe she just liked the song. Who could tell? She had, after all, contracted the queer son of her late brother to sing, a capella and solo, over that brother's open casket, quite dismissing the fact that there had been precious little love lost between father and son.

As to my cousin Athena, wronged mother and betrayed friend: She had neither made eye contact with nor spoken to me since leaving the kitchen table the previous morning, despite sharing the backseat of the Blue Bomb with me from Anna Lee's house all the way to the church. She had also managed to maneuver no fewer than three cousins of mine (whose faces I barely remembered, as an entire generation had been born and received their driver's licenses since I'd last been in the vicinity) between Lucille, Nigel and myself, and her. She had obviously chosen to grieve while maintaining a cool distance from those of us who had conspired to hurt her.

Personally, I wanted nothing so much as to take my cousin by her bony shoulders and shake her until her badly capped teeth clattered like a stenographer on an old Smith-Corona.

Following the song, and the requisite "Amen"s and "Thank you, Jesus"es, the pastor (a tall, blue-black old gentleman with snowy hair — a silent-film Uncle Tom in an incongruously expensive-looking suit) rose to the pulpit. "Lance Joseph Rousseau," he began in the slow, studied cadence affected by ham actors and black Pentecostal preachers, "was a child of this community."

"Yes, he was," agreed someone in the congregation.

"He was a child of this very church home," the pastor continued, eliciting an "Amen." At which point, I switched off. I knew who Lance Joseph Rousseau had been, where he had gone, and exactly who had survived him. I really didn't need the good reverend to tell me. I looked down into my lap at the hastily created funeral program, at the picture of my father on the front of it. The snapshot had been taken shortly after his induction into the army in 1951, before he was shipped off to Korea. It was Aunt Lucille's favorite picture of her brother, and mine. Even in bad photocopy, my father (not yet my father, at this point, of course) is matinee-idol handsome, like Harry Belafonte in *Carmen Jones*, looking not so much like a young soldier as a beautiful young actor *playing* a young soldier. I stared into the forty-year-old image of my father's face and conjured up the most pleasant memory of Lance Rousseau I could recall:

I am just a kid, maybe ten years old. It's Saturday morning and I am lying in bed, not sleeping but not yet ready to relinquish the warm and soft of my bed. And my father comes into the room, climbs into my bed, and lies full-length on top of me, wiggling around and bouncing the bed. "Wake up, Bonie Maronie," he says in a funny little voice, like a man talking through a puppet or reading a bedtime story. "Time's a-wastin'." And I'm laughing and squirming with the deliciousness of it, the weight and warmth of my father on top of me, the feeling of his Saturday-morning beard stubble scraping against my face, the smell of his sour morning breath in my nose.

My father woke me up that way every Saturday morning for a while, for some unremembered period between my being too little and my being too big. And I remember how I missed it when he stopped doing it. But it really isn't the sort of thing a boy could ask his father to do, now is it?

Nigel pulled me back into the still, humid present with the touch of his hand on my leg. "It's time," he whispered. And when I looked up to find the small congregation's faces focused on me, I realized the reverend had said his say and it was now my turn. I took a good, long breath of the musty air and let it out slowly. I moved my aunt's veil aside and kissed her sweet-smelling and properly powdered cheek before rising from my seat.

I took in air through my nostrils and released it though my mouth, as music:

> *Steal away*
> *Steal away*
> *Steal away to Jesus*
> *Steal away*
> *Steal away home*
> *I ain't got long to stay here.*

I heard the murmurs ("Yes, Lord" and "Thank you, Jesus" and "Well?") from behind and to either side of me through that first chorus, even a few voices humming in harmony with me. I heard the "Amen"s of agreement at the end of that chorus: there's nothing like a dead body in the room to point up the layers of truth in the line "I ain't got long to stay here."

Sure, the slave forebears of all of us in that little church house may well have sung the song as a coded message about stealing away north to Canada or across the ocean to Africa. But I'd have bet dollars to doorstops that the home on nearly everyone's mind as I sang was the Eternal Home — the heaven I may or may not have believed in that morning. After all, who among us has long to stay here?

I doubt anyone in the congregation, save Nigel and possibly Athena, could have imagined that I sang not for my father — nor did I particularly believe in stealing away home to Jesus — but for my aunt, because she had asked me to.

And I was singing because I could. Because after oh-so-many months of subsisting on other people's music, music from stereo speakers and radios and my sweet friend Mr. Walkman, I could lift my head, my chest, and my high first tenor and sing,

> *My Lord he calls me*
> *He calls me by the thunder*
> *The trumpet sounds within-a my soul.*

And while it certainly uplifted me, strengthened me to sing that song, it likely would have lifted my rather bruised spirit just as high to sing "Oh Danny Boy" or "My Country 'Tis of Thee" or "Hut-Sut Rawlson on the Rillerah."

Well, maybe not "Hut-Sut Rawlson on the Rillerah."

It certainly didn't hurt matters, as I sang the song my aunt had requested I sing, to feel the long-fingered hand of my cousin Nigel in my own, holding tight in front of God and everybody, the high probability of our being noticed by his mother, any number of relatives close and distant, and the white-headed Reverend What's-his-name, notwithstanding.

I finished my song to a chorus of "Amen"s, gave my cousin's hand a little squeeze, and took my seat.

■

I had to talk to Athena.

She had made it clear that she had no intention of talking to me. She had successfully avoided me at the church and positioned herself as far away from me as possible at the cemetery where my father was lowered into the damp clay amid more tears and more words of comfort by the good reverend. Now, back at the house, where a good-sized group of mourners and sympathizers had gathered bearing covered dishes of spicy, aromatic foods — following the age-old Southern tradition that the recently bereaved should neither go hungry nor be burdened with the chore of cooking their own suppers for at least a couple of weeks — Athena was very obviously keeping as much distance between us as she could while still remaining under the same roof.

I couldn't leave things between us quite this ugly, certainly not without giving peace another chance.

I spotted Athena in the kitchen, pouring Lynn-Yvette Mayall a cup of coffee. She all but dropped the electric percolator to the counter when she noticed me moving purposefully toward her, and bolted like a frightened faun. I "pardon-me-excuse-me"-ed my way through the crowded kitchen, following Athena toward the bathroom. Her latest escape was all but complete when I caught the door with my foot and slipped into the bathroom behind her. I shut the door, hooked it, and stood between it and Athena, arms crossed over my chest like Mr. Clean.

She countered my pose with one of her own, punching her fists into her hips and saying, "What the hell you think you're doing?"

"Theen," I said, uncrossing my arms, "I'm going home in a few hours."

"Good," she said with a little toss of her head.

"Athena..." I reached a hand toward her, but she stepped aside. "We've been too close for too long to ruin it all over something like this."

"Something *like* this?" she said. "Ain't nothin' else like this, Junie."

"Athena, I love you so much." I could feel tears beginning to sting the corners of my eyes. "I thought you loved me. I can't believe you can't, or won't find it within yourself to forgive me this" — I searched the bathroom ceiling for a word — "indiscretion."

"Well, I can't," she said, her too-even teeth clenched. "Not today, anyhow. Maybe later, maybe sometime,

Junie, but not today." She shook her head. "Sure as shit not today."

"For crying out loud, Theena. I thought I knew you. I thought we were friends. What happened to that girl who said to me, 'So what if you're gay, Junie — it makes no difference to me, let's go get a burger'?"

"You're not my child, Junie," she said, pointing a slender index finger in my face. "You're Miss Clara's problem, not mine. Nigel Walker is *my* problem," she said, tapping that finger into the center of her own chest.

"What in the world are you talking about?" I said.

And then suddenly, I knew. This was all about Athena having walked into a roomful of all-but-irrefutable evidence that her son was queer, and needing someone to blame.

And I thought, My God — she's just like Lance. Maybe all parents are just like my late father when it comes to having a gay son.

Oh, woe to the gay sons!

And I said, "I see. So, it's all very well for Cousin Junie to be a cocksucker, but not your Nigel, oh no."

Athena stamped her foot to the faded linoleum floor like child actor of modest talent. "Dammit, Junie, he's my only child."

"And if, heaven forfend, your only child happens to be gay," I said, wiping a tear from my face with the heel of my hand, "then I guess he's just not quite good enough, is he? Not quite everything you'd hoped for in a son. Isn't that right?"

"He's not like you, Junie," Athena said. "He's just a baby. He'll grow out of it."

I refused to address that statement. I said, "Athena, I don't know when I've been so disappointed, in anyone."

"You got your nerve," she said, making a sour face, "calling yourself disappointed with *me.*"

I saw no good reason to take up that point. I shrugged. "You may be right." I unhooked the door, swung it open, and walked out into the hall, where I was immediately set upon by Mr. Freen, wearing a shiny old suit and a sympathetic expression.

"So sorry about your daddy," he said, applying a knotted hand to my shoulder.

"Thank you, sir," I said as Athena brushed past me from behind.

■

"You ready, Cap?" Nigel asked.

"Ready," I said, zipping my suitcase closed on the bed whereon I'd first tasted Nigel's sweet mouth. My father was in the ground and I was ready — well, as ready as I could be without the benefit of hard drugs — to take the air: dressed in one of the chinos-and-alligator-shirt ensembles I liked to travel in, and having recently swallowed a Dramamine and a half.

Athena had left me no choice but to reconcile myself to the fact that she and I would not likely kiss and make up on this visit. The thought of which was bothersome, though hardly unbearable. My own mother and I had remained incommunicado (didn't visit, didn't drop a postcard, didn't pick up the phone) for over a year following one particularly passionate disagreement. Some things, and some people, take time. I had hugged and kissed relatives whose faces I did not remember and accepted sympathy for grief I was none too sure I actually felt. I had sung my song. There was no reason to stay longer.

Except, of course, the young man standing near me with my garment bag thrown over his shoulder and the keys to the Blue Bomb jingling from his fingers, changed from his funeral outfit and into a trademark tank top and jeans. Three days before, I hadn't even known this person, and now I could already feel how much I'd miss him once I'd gone.

When the idea came to me, I didn't stop to consider it, to analyze it, to give it anything resembling conscious thought. As is my all-too-frequent habit, I didn't think before I spoke.

"Nigel," I said, "come with me."

"Shot who?" Nigel said, a funny little half smile on his lips.

"Come with me," I repeated. "Come live with me." It made perfect sense — at the time I said it, anyway. Nigel loved me; the feeling was mutual. How often does this happen in one lifetime? "We could drive back," I went on. "Your mother told me the car was mine if I wanted it."

"Captain," Nigel said, slowly, casting me a sidelong look whose meaning I could not immediately fathom, "I got ... school, come the fall."

"Though you may not think so," I said, "there are schools in California. I can help put you through. I can afford it." And I could. Keith had left me relatively well provided for and, of course, I worked.

Nigel lowered my suit bag from his shoulder and draped it over his arm. "I mean," he said, "I've been accepted at LSU. I've got a partial scholarship, a student loan, and a promise of a part-time job. I've got—" He shrugged, the look on his face broadcasting something very like desperation.

And suddenly, it was as if I had snuck up behind a friend in a public place, slipped my arms around his waist, and kissed him on the side of his neck, only to discover that I'd been mistaken and had accidentally accosted a stranger. I realized what my cousin was trying so hard to tell me without inadvertently destroying me: that he was not yet nineteen god-damn years old. With college, with many more loves, with his entire friggin' life ahead of him. With so much that was years behind me, ahead of him.

I felt old and ridiculous, as if I had offered some lovely young thing all the money in my wallet just to stroke his hair and massage his feet, and had been snickeringly rejected.

If I had thought it remotely possible to bolt from the room, from my cousin's visible discomfort, and from my aunt's house, and to run every step of the way back to Los Angeles with three pieces of luggage in my hands, I would have given it my best shot. As things were, I could only make wildly inarticulate gestures with my hands and stammer, "I'm sorry. I — I don't know why I said that. I—"

Nigel allowed my suit bag to slip from his arm and onto the bed. With a smile so tender I thought I might cry, he lifted one hand toward my face and touched my cheek, just at the cheekbone, with the tips of his long fingers. "Can I come visit on summer vacation?" he said.

I nodded a quick series of up-and-down-up-and-down. "Yes."

Nigel kissed my lips and said, "You know I love you."

I nodded again and said, "Yes."

■

Minutes before boarding time. I sat in the air-conditioned cool of the terminal, in a molded plastic chair seemingly designed for maximum discomfort, perhaps in order to discourage loitering. I held my boarding pass in my hand and the beginnings of a Dramamine fog between my ears. Reaching up to brush a small itch from my nose, I could still smell Aunt Lucille on my fingers from our good-bye hugs at the door of her house. Athena had made a point of avoiding me and we had exchanged no apologies, no farewells. Lucille had said something about "getting that little heifer in here to say good-bye," but I pleaded with her to let Athena be.

"Maybe we'll be able to work this out sometime," I said. "Or not."

"You take care of yourself, baby," she said, almost a whisper.

And I said, "I'll try, ma'am."

Nigel emerged from the men's room across the terminal from where I sat. I watched my cousin walk toward me — the swing of his arms, his long-legged stride, the wonderful way he filled his jeans in the front. And as so many things do, it made me think of a song. I quoted it as Nigel approached.

"'You walk like the angels talk.'"

"I do who?" he said.

I rose from my chair and said, "It's from a song."

We stood and traded grins for at least a full minute before I took my cousin into my arms and we hugged hard, rocking gently from side to side.

"Be happy," he said, reminding me of another boy who'd admonished me in the same way — sweet Lord, nearly twenty years before. A boy I'd loved in high school. And I would have to admit that I'd actually been happy since that time. Intermittently, at least. Which is, I would imagine, considerably better than the national average.

"Do well in school" was the best I could do in reply. I gathered my luggage and started toward the gate.

"I'll write to you," Nigel called to me as I started away. I smiled, not so much because I actually believed a busy college freshman would find the time to write letters to his nearly twice-his-age cousin half a continent away, but because I knew that at the time at least, he really meant to.

I didn't turn around, but raised my right hand and waved the palm-open, finger-wiggling backward wave

I'd used from time to time since first seeing Liza Minelli do it near the end of *Cabaret*. I think it's rather a smart little gesture. And there was no real need for Nigel to see the tears on my face, tears which I knew would either quick-dry or merge with the sweat that would break the moment I stepped out of the air-conditioned terminal and out into the unbearably hot, humid air, walking the heat-softened tarmac toward another airplane which only I seemed to realize had no business attempting to leave the ground.